"You're really not going to answer that?"

"Nope."

"At least confirm that I'm the cute guy?"

"You're not," Brooke said. "I was talking about the guy who helped me take my groceries to the car the other day. He even called me 'ma'am,' which made me feel old but also made me feel kind of fancy."

She twisted her shoulder in an endearing way, and Tyler smiled. How could he be so delighted by her? She drew him in—no, locked him in, really—and he was so enamored that he'd handed her the key.

"You should stop doing this," he said, meaning to tease, but his tone was serious.

"What?"

"Being...so you."

She studied him. "I would be offended if it weren't for that look on your face. It's telling me you're actually complimenting me."

"Yeah." His hand lifted to twirl the ends of her hair around his finger. He stopped when he reached halfway. "Sorry. I..."

He didn't finish, and she reached up and caught his hand. "You know what I think would solve a lot of this tension? If we kissed."

Dear Reader,

Over the eighteen books I've written, I've been open to trying almost every contemporary romance trope. And yet Brooke and Tyler's story is the first time I've explored amnesia. In typical Therese fashion, I complicated the trope, then added some more complications (oops?). So now our hero can't ask our heroine about their past, which she's seemingly ignoring; after all, he can't broach such personal topics with his new boss!

As with all my romances, expect emotion, banter and, most important, hope. Love is the best way we can remind ourselves of the goodness in the world. I hope this book does that for you!

Love,

Therese

Awakened by the CEO's Kiss

Therese Beharrie

HARLEQUIN®

Romance™

Recycling programs
for this product may
not exist in your area.

ISBN-13: 978-1-335-40672-9

Awakened by the CEO's Kiss

Copyright © 2021 by Therese Beharrie

This edition published by arrangement with Harlequin Books S.A.

For questions and comments about the quality of this book,
please contact us at CustomerService@Harlequin.com.

Harlequin Enterprises ULC
22 Adelaide St. West, 40th Floor
Toronto, Ontario M5H 4E3, Canada
www.Harlequin.com

Printed in U.S.A.

Being an author has always been **Therese Beharrie**'s dream. But it was only when the corporate world loomed during her final year at university that she realized how soon she wanted that dream to become a reality. So she got serious about her writing and now writes books she wants to see in the world featuring people who look like her for a living. When she's not writing, she's spending time with her husband and dogs in Cape Town, South Africa. She admits that this is a perfect life and is grateful for it.

Books by Therese Beharrie

Harlequin Romance

Billionaires for Heiresses

Second Chance with Her Billionaire
From Heiress to Mom

Tempted by the Billionaire Next Door
Surprise Baby, Second Chance
Her Festive Flirtation
Island Fling with the Tycoon
Her Twin Baby Secret
Marrying His Runaway Heiress
His Princess by Christmas

Visit the Author Profile page at Harlequin.com.

To my incredible family.

The love I have for you keeps me hopeful. Thank you for reminding me of the world's beauty.

Praise for Therese Beharrie

CHAPTER ONE

FOR THE SECOND time in his life Tyler Murphy was staring at the most beautiful woman he had ever seen.

The first time had been five years ago, at a coffee shop around the corner from the hospital. He had been visiting his sister, who'd just given birth to his nephew, and he had been dealing with some…stuff. Mainly the fact that his mother, who had passed away months before that, wouldn't get to meet her first grandchild. The woman who had prized family so much wouldn't get to see hers expand.

He'd needed some space from the hospital. And there had been Brooke. Standing at the counter, staring at the menu with a dazed look on her face.

He thought about that day a lot. The days after, too—that week they'd spent together. The sadness that had lurked in her eyes even when she was smiling. How often she would trail off when she spoke, as if she had forgotten what she was saying. She would always beam at him after, especially if he prompted her, and he'd put it down as one of her quirks.

Those memories were all he had of her. Her first name—only her first name—and his memories. It hadn't mattered then. He had known she was the type of person who picked up litter when she saw it on the street. Who allowed elderly people ahead of her in a queue. She hoped for a world where people were kinder, less self-centred. She didn't like intolerance, and she had told him about the times she'd stepped in when she'd witnessed it.

But her name and his memories hadn't been enough for him to find her. He'd discovered that at the end of the week when she'd disappeared. They hadn't shared any information about where they lived, who their families were. They hadn't even exchanged contact details. It was as if they'd purposely avoided it. As if *she* had purposely avoided it.

He might have thought it dramatic if he hadn't been staring at her now, waiting for her to recognise him.

He got nothing.

'You're not Tia Murphy,' she said, her voice a frustratingly adorable lilt of confusion.

'No, I'm Tyler Murphy.' *Which you already know. But I guess if we're playing this game...* 'I'll be helping you out for the next—'

He didn't get the chance to continue. Brooke let out a cry as her body bumped against the door. Seconds later, the door opened wider. He didn't catch what flew past them, but he knew it was some kind of animal.

'No!' she shouted. 'Mochi, you come back here *right now*!'

She ran down the three steps that led to the front lawn, before bolting towards what Tyler could now see was a dog. He didn't think she'd expected to chase after a dog. Or maybe she had; he wasn't proficient in what kind of clothes people who required housekeepers wore.

Sure, technically, he could be one of those people, but his mother would have killed him. If he'd got a housekeeper now, she'd probably become undead for the sole purpose of killing him.

And, since he wasn't 'one of those people,' for all he knew Brooke's silky nightgown and flip-flops were standard attire.

Watching her running after a dog in that outfit lightened some of the tension he felt, but it couldn't eradicate it completely. In fact, it complicated things. In the days they'd spent together, he hadn't once seen this much of her. Now he could add the strength of her arms, the width of her thighs, to what he'd been missing.

Get it together, Murphy.

Brooke was now his boss. Indirectly, since

he was standing in for his sister. But still... He needed to keep things professional. The situation was precarious enough without the added complication of him knowing Brooke.

Except... Was she pretending that week hadn't happened? Or did she not remember it? He did, because he had never been so attracted to anyone. Not any of the women he'd dated, though there had only been a few over the years. None of them stood out. But he'd thought he and Brooke had shared something. If not physically, emotionally. They had been *friends*.

And she didn't remember that?

Was he so out of touch that he'd made up their connection?

He exhaled. Now was not the time to dwell on the past. Especially when the present was providing enough distraction.

The dog was having the time of its life. It was a collie cross of some kind, with glossy black fur and brown and white paws. It barked at the woman frequently, as if taunting her. It was probably taunting her because it barked every time she paused to take a breath. When she started chasing it again, it zoomed past her, literally running circles around her.

He wanted to be the better person and help her. And he would. But he'd watch for a while longer before he did. It wasn't something he was proud of, but it did offer him a measure of satisfaction. As did the steam he was sure he could see coming from her head.

He walked down the steps, put his fingers in his mouth and whistled.

'Mochi,' he called, lowering to his haunches. 'Come on over here. Introduce yourself.'

In no time at all the dog was in front of him, wagging its tail enthusiastically as it licked Tyler's face and smelled his clothing.

'How did you do that?' Brooke demanded, walking over to him. 'I've had him for two weeks and never—*never*—has calling him worked.'

'You need to call with authority,' Tyler replied absently, smiling when the dog lay on his back for a belly rub. 'Dogs need to know who the alpha of their pack is. If they think they can take advantage of you, they will.'

'Ah,' she said, nodding.

Tyler picked the dog up and tucked him under his arm.

'Well, thank you so much… Tyler, you said your name was?'

'Yes.'

'Thank you, Tyler.' She took the dog from him. 'Let's go inside so you can explain why you're here and not Tia. Don't worry,' she added casually, 'I'll be sure to remember my *authority* during our conversation.'

Tyler opened his mouth to reply, but she hadn't waited for one. Good thing. He had no real answer, and if he came up with something on the fly he'd surely put his foot in it again.

'I assume the fact that you share a surname with the person who's supposed to be here is significant,' she said, when they were both inside the house.

She closed the door and put down the dog, which immediately went to Tyler. He didn't dare look at it.

'Explain.'

She folded her arms, appearing oblivious to the fact that the movement might, in someone with less self-control, draw attention to her chest. The way her nightgown formed a V at her cleavage, creating soft semi-circles of flesh, might, again, in someone with less self-control, cause desire to shoot straight to a part of the body inappropriate for a professional setting.

That someone was obviously not him. He had plenty of self-control. Exemplified by how he was focusing on her face, not her cleavage. Focusing on those brown eyes that wore fury and command as though they were cloaks. On the perfectly formed eyebrows, dark like the hair pulled into a bun at the top of her head, highlighting sharp, almost regal cheekbones. On the full lashes that made her the perfect model for mascara, though he knew she hadn't used any. On the plump pink lips that were currently in a thin line, like a disapproving teacher.

He had never, not once in his life, had a teacher fantasy, but he was beginning to see the appeal.

Had he implied that this woman had no authority? No—he'd *said* it. Foolishly, considering she held his sister's employment in her hands. Stupidly, considering she wore only nightwear and somehow still had an aura of power coming off her as if it was a particularly potent brand of perfume.

He was already enthralled, already aroused, and they'd spent all of fifteen minutes together. How the hell was he going to get through a month?

Distance. Right, yes. Distance and professionalism. Two characteristics he generally displayed without much effort.

He cleared his throat. 'Tia Murphy is my sister. Unfortunately, she won't be able to fulfil this commitment due to unforeseen circumstances.'

'The agency sent you instead?'

He hesitated. 'No.'

'Care to elaborate?'

'They…they don't know.'

'So you're telling me I have a random man in my house who hasn't been verified by the agency I've already paid?'

Mochi whined at his feet, as if in warning.

'That's not how I would phrase it…' Tyler said carefully.

'How *would* you phrase it?' Her voice was dangerously cool. 'I'm very interested in knowing. I could do with a concise explanation, too, since I have to leave for work in—' She broke off as her eyes fluttered to the clock on the wall behind him. 'Crap. I leave in fifteen minutes.' She narrowed her eyes. 'Should I trust a random man in my home while I change?'

'We've been alone for a while, and I've been perfectly respectable. Plus, your dog trusts me.'

She studied him. Didn't at all seemed convinced. She looked at Mochi. 'Make sure he doesn't steal anything,' she instructed, before walking up the stairs without a further word.

He looked at the dog. 'I'm not sure she likes me.'

Mochi only tilted his head.

This was a confusing situation on multiple levels. For one, Brooke Jansen hadn't expected to be dressed as though she were preparing for a boudoir photo shoot when she met her temporary housekeeper for the first time. But Mochi had woken her up and refused to leave her alone until she gave him something.

What he'd wanted, she didn't know. She'd

barely managed her morning routine before he'd started barking. Sharp, piercing barks that demanded attention. Then the doorbell had rang, and Mochi had escaped. She wouldn't be surprised if he'd been planning it since he'd woken her up.

The second thing was the man she'd found on her doorstep. She had been…surprised. It wasn't that she thought he couldn't be a housekeeper. Her brain had just taken a moment to reconcile his sheer physical size with what the job required. He looked more suited to doing something that required strength. Like carrying heavy items from one place to another.

For a brief moment she considered how many tasks she could find that would allow him to do that. And would allow her to watch.

Very quickly after that thought she gathered her wits. After chiding them for their inappropriate behaviour, she realised he wasn't meant to be here.

Which brought her to a third confusing aspect: *he wasn't meant to be here.*

That was something she needed to sort out. Honestly, she was annoyed. She had hired a housekeeper to help her since her focus was almost entirely on work these days. She didn't need a housekeeper to add to her problems. Especially a sexy housekeeper.

Sexy? She had entertained, however briefly, the idea of watching him work, but *sexy*?

What was going on? She hadn't cared about any of that since Kian had died. She wasn't even sure she cared now.

Except she might care. Why else was she wearing a top that made her breasts look appealing under a stylish blazer, with jeans that did impressive things for her butt? And why was she now slipping on a pair of heels, putting on more accessories than she had in months, doing elaborate make-up? Her hair was due for a wash, so the best she could do was put it back into the bun, forcing any stray pieces into place with gel.

But that was *all* she was doing.

The bare minimum, really.

Ignoring any thoughts to the contrary, she made her way downstairs. The smell of coffee hit her first, before she realised Tyler wasn't in the hall where she'd left him. She hadn't really expected him to stay there. Though the fact that she was surprised he wasn't there now proved otherwise.

Her eyes swept over the house. Nothing seemed out of place, which was a positive. She wouldn't have been impressed with herself if she'd let a criminal into her home. Less so if she'd been attracted to the criminal.

Not that she was attracted to him. She could

objectively notice a man's attractiveness without being attracted to him.

Her thoughts stalled when she saw Tyler in the kitchen though. Her heart skipped and time… Well, it did what time always did. It moved on. So slowly that she could hear every tick of the clock, as if it were trying to tell her something.

But that couldn't possibly be. What would it have to tell her? And why was that question more important than all the others she had? About Tyler looking as if he belonged in her kitchen as much as he did carrying very heavy things from one place to the next.

'I made coffee. It's in a takeaway cup.' He nodded his head to the kitchen table. 'With a toasted cheese sandwich you can have for breakfast.' He studied her. 'I assume you haven't had breakfast?'

A restless sensation slithered up her spine, sliding its hands over her shoulders and settling over her heart. She didn't know how much of it was surprise and how much of it was concern. She hadn't had someone take care of her this way in the longest time. Her brother was a constant presence in her life, and he would have, certainly, if she let him. But she rarely did. Accepting the dog he'd given her because he was worried about her had been a concession because she knew that.

Now there was a stranger doing things for her. Was she supposed to accept it?

'You're overthinking things,' he told her, his tone curt. 'I'm here to do a job. This is part of it.'

'Except this isn't your job, is it? You're standing in for your sister.'

'She and I have the same skills.'

'But you haven't been vetted by the agency. For all I know you're a master criminal, preparing to rob me of everything I own.'

He snorted. 'Your imagination is something.'

She opened her mouth to reply, but he continued before she could.

'My name is Tyler Murphy. Look me up. I own an online education company. We provide courses aimed at older students, accredited by the government. There are multiple articles about me, including a detailed personal history, all of which should address your concerns about me being a master criminal. Among other things,' he added coolly.

She had no idea what he meant by that.

Eyeing him suspiciously, she took out her phone and typed in his name. Everything he said was true.

'This doesn't make what you and your sister are doing okay.'

'Believe me, if there was another choice we wouldn't be doing it.'

Oddly, she believed him. She didn't approve, but she understood. She would have stood in for her brother in a heartbeat if he'd needed her—although she doubted she would be able to do Dom's job as a police officer.

'Fine. I won't tell the agency, but obviously you're on probation.'

'Obviously,' he said blandly.

She lifted her brows. 'Since you have your own company, you might not know how to interact with an employer. Generally you don't sass them. Nor do you imply that they don't have authority in their own homes, with their own pets.'

He had the grace to wince. 'I'm sorry about that. I realised it was a mistake as soon as I said it.'

'No, you realised it was a mistake as soon as I pointed it out.'

She hadn't fully appreciated his face until that moment, when his mouth curved into an almost-smile. It softened his eyes, edging the colour from brown into green in a startlingly contrary way. Or perhaps it wasn't a softening, but a sparkle. An acknowledgement of sass and truth that was delightful on the hard angles of his face. It cast a light on his stormy features—on the dark brows and lashes, the tight pursing of his lips—and she wasn't sure she liked it.

Liar, said an inner voice.

Mind your business, she mentally replied.

She couldn't say much more than that.

'You're right.'

'I know,' she said primly, before looking down at Mochi. He was sitting calmly on the floor between them, panting blissfully with his legs crossed. 'You're a show-off, Mochi.'

'Why do you say that?' Tyler asked.

His eyes were sparkling with vague amusement now. Something prickled in her body.

She cleared her throat. 'He's very well behaved around people, but as soon as you leave he'll do what he did outside.'

'Play?'

'Yeah, if you mean it in a play *me* kind of way.'

'I didn't, but I guess that works.'

He smiled now. A full smile. An easy smile. The kind of smile that made her think of summer and driving through the city. With the sun streaming through the windows, heating her face, her arms, her legs. She could almost hear the music through the speakers.Could almost feel Kian's fingers twined through hers—

Her heart stopped.

For a few seconds, her heart just stopped.

Because she'd looked at one man, this man in front of her, and thought about her dead husband. And that didn't feel right. It felt complicated. She didn't even want to think it through.

His smile disappeared.

'Tia's briefed me on what you require,' he said formally.

She wondered at the change. There was no possible way he could know what she had been thinking.

'I understand what my responsibilities will be in the coming weeks. And I am good with dogs. As you can see.'

He lowered his hand to his side. Mochi immediately stood, placing his head directly beneath Tyler's fingers.

Brooke tilted her head. 'Neat trick.'

'It's not a trick, Ms Jansen.' He gave her a cocky smile.

Why did the man have so many variations of his smile? And why did they all have a familiar shimmer of awareness going through her?

'I need time to think through this situation,' she said, though she hadn't been prepared to say it. 'I'll let you know if you can come back.'

'You're not hiring me?' he asked, indignation a hoarse undertone in his voice.

'Not yet, Mr Murphy.' She picked up her coffee and the sandwich and nodded her head towards the door. 'Now, do you mind? I'm already late for work.'

CHAPTER TWO

'How did it go?'

Tyler pressed the phone to his ear with his shoulder, deliberating on how he should answer. He could tell the truth: the woman Tia had asked him to work for was the same woman he'd formed a friendship with five years ago. He thought about her often, especially when he was considering dating, and those thoughts usually put him off dating. After all, how was he meant to establish a connection like that with someone else?

Of course today, he'd discovered that connection was one-sided. It had kept him from asking Brooke why she was ignoring him. If he really had been the only one to experience their connection, it would be embarrassing to demand that she address their past. He had his pride, damn it. And he was nursing his wounds now, using the sting to establish boundaries that would keep him from doing something stupid.

Like beg her to remember him and their week together.

Wasn't it as special as I thought? he'd probably ask. *Didn't we share something?*

But that would only lead to more stupidity, as it had today. When he'd insulted Brooke, treated her coolly, and jeopardised Tia's job. Tia was more important than his hurt feelings. He couldn't allow those feelings to motivate his behaviour again. He would have to ignore the past, just as Brooke was doing.

No, he couldn't tell Tia any of that. So he lied.

'It went great.'

'Yeah?'

The relief embedded in that word made him glad he lied. She was under a lot of pressure. The least he could do was reassure her.

Until she finds out you're lying and she loses her job at the agency.

That wouldn't be ideal. Especially when she was desperately trying to *keep* her job, hence him filling in for her in the first place.

'I've already used all my leave, Ty. If I tell them I need to take care of Nyle again, they'll fire me. And you know I need this job,' she'd said when she'd asked for his help.

'Yeah, I know,' he'd replied, 'because you won't let me help you.'

'Financially,' she'd emphasised. 'But I do know of another way you can help me…'

How could he have said no then?

Plus, his job allowed him to work remotely. Hell, his company was independent enough that he could take a couple of weeks' leave. Which was likely why he was getting so restless professionally. In its current state, it no longer provided a challenge. Expansion, on the other hand—

As he had been doing for the last month, he stopped the thought in its tracks. There was no point in indulging it. He wouldn't be taking the opportunity. It didn't matter that it was an incredible opportunity that had seemingly come out of the blue.

He had been at a function at one of the universities his company was partnered with when he'd been approached by the CEO of a company similar to his own. Apparently, he'd heard about what Learn It, Tyler's company, was doing in South Africa, and wanted a merger since he was doing the same in the UK.

Tyler had imagined the possibilities—and he *would* only imagine the possibilities.

There was no way he would leave Tia and Nyle to fend for themselves. They were family, and his mother had taught him he should never abandon family. Drilled it into him, really, after his father had left.

It was ironic that his father's departure had been because of a business opportunity, too. Tyler could almost understand it now. Could see the temptation of it. Except *he* loved his family more than he loved ambition or success. He wouldn't leave for either of them.

'How's Nyle doing?' he asked, mentally shifting gears.

'He still has a fever, but he doesn't feel bad enough to stop complaining about the rash.' Tia exhaled. 'He had the vaccine... I don't understand why he still got chickenpox.'

'It's common enough.' Tyler had done a lot of research to confirm that. 'And it'll be less severe because he was vaccinated.' He paused. 'Tia, you did your best. Stuff like this happens.'

'I know. I know.'

She would still be hard on herself, though. She had been for the last five years. As if being hard on herself would somehow make up for the fact that her boyfriend had left without so much as a word before she'd even found out she was pregnant. When she had found out, she'd done everything she could to find him. She'd even asked Tyler to hire a private investigator.

The investigator had found him pretty quickly. He'd been living six hours away, with his wife and three kids.

Tia hadn't known a thing about any of it, but

she'd admonished herself as if she'd made the choice to get involved with him deliberately. She'd informed him she was pregnant, got the confirmation she hadn't really needed that he didn't want anything to do with her, and prepared to become a single parent.

Tyler liked to think Tia had him, but the truth was she barely asked him for anything. When she did ask him, it was because she had no other option. It was her pride—their mother had raised them with an abundance of it—though heaven only knew why that pride included him. They were family.

But this wasn't about him; it was about Tia. He needed to respect that.

Sharp barking interrupted his thoughts.

'What is...? Ty, did you take in another foster dog?'

He didn't appreciate the accusation. So, again, he found himself lying. 'No.'

'I can hear a dog barking.'

'It's the TV.'

'You're a terrible liar.'

Not about everything.

'You say that like it's a bad thing.'

'You need to stop taking in stray dogs,' Tia replied. 'You're getting a reputation.'

'Again—you say it like it's a bad thing.'

'I say it like a woman who knows there are

liars and con people in the world. If someone ever wanted to set you up, they'd just need to use a dog and—'

'No one is going to set me up using a dog.'

'You don't know.'

'I do. Besides,' he continued, hoping to distract from her concern, 'this one was curled up on the side of the road. I couldn't leave her there.'

Tia muttered something that sounded suspiciously like, *'How come you keep finding dogs, but not a woman to bring home?'*

'What was that?'

'I hope your tetanus shot is up to date,' she said.

'Since you ask me that every time, you already know the answer. Now, do I need to bring anything over for you and Nyle?'

It took some cajoling, but eventually Tia agreed to have him bring over some groceries. But only if he left them at the front door since he'd only recently got his chickenpox vaccine. An oversight by their mother which, considering she had already passed away when they'd discovered it, they would never know the reason for.

The only reason they knew now was because Tia had insisted they check their vaccine status. She'd only cared about hers so she could be prepared, but since Tyler had at first offered to look after Nyle while she worked, she'd insisted he check, too. It was one of the few times Tia's micro-parenting had worked out.

'Want to come with me?' he asked his new dog.

He'd temporarily named her June until the owner came forward, but he suspected it would be while. He'd put up fliers at the local vet clinics and in the area he'd found her since she didn't have a chip.

June's tail wagged so fast he thought she might sprain it.

'Okay, okay, let's go.'

He left her in the car when he went to get Tia's groceries, but decided to take her for a walk once the shopping was done. The store wasn't far from Tia's place, so he left his car in the car park. Twenty minutes later, the goods had been delivered and he was on his way back.

Then he saw his new maybe-boss.

'Mochi, I swear if you don't stop pulling, I'm going to—'

Brooke broke off as she passed a couple walking their own dog. Neither of them seemed as annoyed as she was. But then, their miniature fluff ball of a dog seemed nowhere near as passionate as Mochi, who was pulling at the leash so hard it felt as though he wanted to win a race.

Brooke half-ran, half-stumbled to keep up. She

was about to give Mochi another talking-to—
because that was truly working *so* well—when
someone spoke.

'Are you walking Mochi or is Mochi walking you?'

Her mouth was dry long before she met his
eyes. When she did, she felt a small jolt. It was
recognition, but a deeper kind than what meeting
him a few hours ago should have brought. She
brushed it off. It was probably because he was attractive. And, contrary to what she had told herself that morning, she *was* attracted to him. To
the faint smirk that she so badly wanted to flick
off his face. To the slight folds between his eyebrows that made his face look stormy once again.

What was she supposed to do with all this information?

'Tyler.'

She stopped, struggling to keep Mochi back
when he, too, recognised Tyler. Tyler looked
more thrilled to see the dog than he did her. Not
that she cared, of course.

He had his own dog with him. It was mixed
breed, and sat patiently at his side, staring at the
scene as if it had never once in its life misbe-
haved.

'What are you doing here?' he asked, dropping
to give Mochi some love. Mochi allowed it for all
of ten seconds before moving to sniff Tyler's dog.

'Is this area reserved for people who aren't me?'

He gave her a dark look as he straightened. 'It's a little far from home.'

It was, but this was where her brother had told her the SPCA had picked Mochi up when they'd got news about a stray dog in the park. Brooke thought the area might comfort him. She wasn't sure about that, but it did seem to excite him.

She told none of this to Tyler, especially since it was fairly self-evident why she was there, apart from it being far from home. The park was large and surrounded by trees. There was a path for those who wanted to walk, and in the middle, a play area with some benches. It was a pretty standard park in a Cape Town suburb, and it was a great place to walk a dog.

She didn't know why she was resisting telling Tyler the truth. None of it was incriminating. But the thought of sharing it with him felt intimate in a way she couldn't explain.

She shrugged. 'Mochi likes it here.'

'How exactly did you figure that out?'

Oh, she'd walked into that one.

Instead of answering, she deflected. 'Who's your friend?' She gestured to the dog beside him.

'This is… Well, I'm not sure.'

'You're not sure?' she repeated slowly.

'She's a stray. Or she might be. Again, I'm not sure.'

She found his uncertainty strangely refreshing.

'I found her on the side of the road. She doesn't have a chip, so she might be a stray, but she was in good condition. Well-fed, clean, and she seems trained.'

'So let me get this straight: you picked up a stray dog…' *Of course* a man who looked like him would be partial to picking up stray dogs. Why would the universe make things easy? 'And it's the perfect dog?'

'Well, I didn't say…' He looked down, smiled.

It was a fond smile this time. A gooey smile. Urgh, she hated his range.

'Yeah, she's pretty perfect,' he said.

'Of course she is.'

'What does that mean?'

'Nothing.'

'Please, tell me.' It sounded strangely demanding.

'It means… Well, you finding a perfect stray dog seems consistent with what I know about you.'

'What you know about me?' he repeated, his voice hard. Too hard.

'I'm sorry, that was inappropriate. I shouldn't have implied…' She trailed off when she saw his frown. 'Look, we've spent less than an hour together and yet somehow we've ended up on each other's bad sides.'

'Less than an hour, huh?' he asked, a wry twist to his mouth. 'Is that just today, or are you speaking about for ever?'

'I… I don't know what you mean.'

'Of course you don't.'

She stared at him. At this confusing man who inspired more emotion in her than anyone else had in years. Since Kian had died, she'd rarely felt anything but ambivalence towards men.

To be fair, that was pretty much how she felt about everything since she'd become a widow. The years after the car accident that had taken her husband's life—and a limited part of her memory—were a blur of neither high nor low emotions. She had moved on from it. As much as she could, considering what she'd lost.

She didn't mind losing the memories so much. The doctors had told her it was trauma, physical and emotional. She'd been in an accident; she'd lost her husband. In light of that, the days between his death and funeral wasn't all that much to lose. She remembered only parts of them. Flashes of emotion or scenes. But for the most part, it was lost to her.

Whenever she wanted to mourn it, she would remember that she'd lost her husband. She'd mourn something bigger then.

'I shouldn't have said that,' he said. 'I apologise.'

'I don't quite know what you're apologising

for,' she replied after a beat, 'but I'd rather we move on from it. Especially if you're going to work for me.'

'I'm going to work for you?'

His smile was brighter than she'd seen it. She took a step back, as if she were afraid she would burn.

Oh, you're afraid, all right.

'Yes,' she said curtly. Damn her thoughts. Damn her emotions. 'Don't screw it up.'

He was still grinning when she walked away.

CHAPTER THREE

TYLER COULDN'T FAULT his sister for being too proud to accept help when he had some of that pride, too.

Some? a voice in his head scoffed.

Fine. He had a healthy amount of pride.

It had been the reason he'd got into a fight over a girl when he was at school. He hadn't been able to let go his rival's flirting with his girlfriend, even though he'd known his mother would kill him for it. And it was why he didn't have a relationship with his father. The man had abandoned his family for a *job*. It hadn't started out that way, of course, but what did that matter when that was how it ended?

Today, his pride was the reason he had taken a more…formal approach to his first full day of work at Brooke's.

'Oh.' Her eyes widened when she opened the door, scanning him as if she were a metal detector at the airport. 'You're…um…' She heaved out a breath. 'I shouldn't, as your employer, comment on your attire. Or should I? Honestly, I've never had a housekeeper before, and it feels a bit more personal than… No, you know what? I should keep this professional.'

She stopped rambling when she saw the way he was looking at her. He couldn't have said which way that was. He was reluctantly charmed, even if he did now see the flaw in his plan—and his pride.

'A suit is hardly the most sensible attire for a housekeeping position, Mr Murphy.'

Her spine had straightened; her tone was clipped. It charmed him even more. Perhaps because it was clear he had some effect on her. He hadn't worn a suit for that reason. He'd just wanted to make a good impression since he hadn't been on his best behaviour the day before. Witnessing that effect now made the embarrassment worth it.

Because *of course* a suit wasn't the best outfit to wear for a housekeeping position. He must have known that on some level because he had a change of clothing with him.

Maybe he *had* worn the suit to see how it would affect her. And if he had, he couldn't call his pride healthy. It wasn't healthy to figure out if a woman he'd met five years ago was affected by him when she was pretending she didn't remember him. It was stubborn. Idiotic. Childish.

More so when he was this pleased at her response.

'I wanted to show you I'm serious about being here,' he said.

'Do you have a change of clothing?'

'I do.'

She lifted chin. 'Well, then. I suppose that's good.'

He didn't give in to the smile at the reluctant comment. Only walked in when she opened the door wider and said, 'Come inside.'

He shrugged off his jacket and turned to ask if she had a coat rack. He found her staring at him. 'Is everything okay?' he asked.

'Yes. Of course.' Her face flushed. 'I was just wondering what you were thinking.'

'I've already told you.'

'I think you're lying.'

'Why would I do that?'

'Because this job involves cleaning and making sure my dog doesn't destroy the house. It hardly requires a suit.'

'You don't think people who clean deserve to take pride in their appearance by wearing something like this?'

Her mouth opened for a solid few seconds before she replied. 'That's not what I said. Or meant.'

'Isn't it?'

'Of course not. I meant...' She trailed off.

Started again. 'When you start a job, you dress for the job. The time to impress is during the first meeting. Or the interview.'

'I believe the time to impress is every day you show up.'

She studied him. Took in the curve of his mouth that he could no longer keep in. Rolled her eyes. 'I can't believe that you run a company of one hundred and fifty people with your level of maturity.'

His brows lifted. 'Been looking me up?'

She didn't reply to that. 'I'll walk you through what I need you to do today.'

He followed her, though this time he hid his smile. He wasn't that big an idiot.

She showed him where everything was, explaining what she wanted quickly and concisely. It was a good thing his mother hadn't coddled him. She'd raised both him and Tia to have the necessary skills to survive. He knew how to clean, how to cook, how to do laundry. When he was growing up, he'd cleaned his room every day, the house once a week. He'd alternated with Tia on cooking, except on the days his mother hadn't had to work, which hadn't been all that often. As for laundry… His mother had flat-out refused to wash a teenage boy's dirty clothes.

'You good with everything?' she asked when she was done.

'Yeah. I'm good. Where's Mochi?'

She brushed a strand of hair from her face. It was in a long, sleek ponytail at the base of her skull, with a few pieces falling around her face. It went perfectly with the outfit she wore. A floral dress that flared at her hips in a whimsical way that still managed to look professional.

He wanted to take her hand and ask her to spin around. He wanted to hear her laugh breathlessly as she did so, embarrassed that he'd asked, but still wanting to please him.

He hated himself for it. For the fact that *he* wanted to please *her* because she made his heart thud and she clearly didn't feel the same way.

'He's with my brother for the day,' she answered, not meeting his eyes.

'Did something happen?'

'No. I… My brother has dogs. And a kid. And I think Mochi's happier there than he is here, so I thought… It's your first day. I thought I wouldn't let him bother you.'

'He's not a bother,' he said automatically. Then paused. 'You don't think Mochi is happy here?'

'It's not that he isn't happy here…but he's happier elsewhere.' She lifted her hands in an awkward little gesture. 'I think maybe he's happier with someone else.'

'So you don't think he's happy here *or* happy with you?'

'When you say it like that it makes me sound like I'm delusional.' She gave a self-conscious laugh.

'Brooke,' he said slowly, 'I'm not sure why you think your dog doesn't like you, but—'

'Besides the obvious behaviour problems?'

'Behaviour problems are a result of many things, and training helps with almost all of those things. But honestly, it sounds like you don't think he likes *you*. As in, you as a person?'

The vulnerability on her face reminded him of the day they'd met. Of the days after. It was an expression that would come and go in between smiles and laughs. Sometimes those smiles and laughs had been hard-won, but that had made them seem worth more.

He'd been naïve. That much was clear, based on how badly he'd misinterpreted their 'connection.' But now he could see that his naivety went deeper than he'd initially thought. He'd never once attributed Brooke's vulnerability to self-doubt. No—not self-doubt. Something deeper. Something more complicated.

What was it? And why did he want to know so badly?

'I have good instincts, Tyler. And I trust them.' She exhaled and smoothed the front of her dress down. 'Anyway. I'll see you after work. Or I won't.'

She walked to the kitchen and came back with a set of keys.

'You can use this to get in and out. When I'm not here in the morning, I'll leave a list of the things I need done on the kitchen counter. And that's it. Any questions?'

'No, thanks. I'm good.'

'Great. Then I guess I'll see you when I see you.'

With a curve of her mouth that he could hardly call a smile, she grabbed her things from a small table at the base of the staircase and left him alone. He stared after her for a while, then began his new job.

He started in the kitchen on the ground floor. It was a large, modern room, with light coming in from windows on one side and a glass door on the other. The door led to an outside area that was neatly decorated, with a large pot plant surrounded by two chairs. He went to wipe down the outside furniture, but completely forgot that task when he turned to his left.

It was a garden. A *gigantic* garden. With trees and flowers and a little pond all in one space.

When his business had started doing well, he'd bought himself a house. He'd actually wanted to buy one for his mother, but she'd refused. They'd fought about it for months, and in the end he'd bought the house he'd wanted to buy her for himself, so at least she'd get to experience it.

But buying something this extravagant hadn't even occurred to him.

He should have expected it. Brooke's house was in a notoriously wealthy neighbourhood in Cape Town. The house itself was enormous, and from what he'd seen on the inside, it had earned its place in the area.

But this… This was more than simply expensive. It was art.

There was a patio edged by wooden pillars. Between the pillars were three comfortable-looking couches with red cushioning surrounding a small round table. The table held a candle and some fresh flowers that had clearly been taken from the garden.

White stones led from the patio to a larger outdoor area and through trees in an S-shaped path that eventually looped around and led back. At regular steps of the path was a larger slab of stone to walk on. In the middle of the garden was the pond, with water lilies and actual, real-life fish causing the surface to ripple.

For the first time he noticed the bridge that went from one side of the pond to the other. As he walked the area, he saw that some of the larger trees had benches beneath them. One of them had a swing. And by the end of his exploration, he was wondering what the hell Brooke did to be able to afford this kind of artistry.

When he eventually went back to the kitchen to clean, he tried to use the task to distract himself from that question. But the problem with cleaning was that it gave him time to think. It always had; it was part of the reason he liked it so much. The fact that it was giving him that time now though, when he distinctly did not want it, felt like a betrayal.

So as he cleaned the white marble countertops and backsplashes, did the dishes, polished the wooden cupboards, his mind kept spinning on that question. The same thing happened as he washed the windows and the glass door, cleaned the oven and the microwave, vacuumed and mopped the floors.

He was tired of thinking by the time he moved to the dining room, where the most beautiful wooden dining table he'd ever seen sat on a beige carpet in front of a rustic fireplace.

And on the mantel of that fireplace was a picture of Brooke in the arms of a man.

She was wearing a wedding dress.

CHAPTER FOUR

WHEN BROOKE GOT to Dom's that evening, Mochi wagged his tail, which her brother said meant he liked her.

'You sound like Tyler,' she said, rolling her eyes.

'Tyler?' Dom asked. 'Who's that?'

'Oh…um…' She cursed her skin when it started going warm. 'He's my new housekeeper.'

Dom stared at her. 'Okay, I have a lot of questions.'

'I imagine you do,' she replied dryly. 'You might as well ask them. I know you won't stop bugging me until I answer.'

He didn't even bother pretending it wouldn't happen. 'Why do you need a housekeeper?'

'I don't have a spouse to help me, like you have Sierra.'

He gave her a look. 'That's not going to work on me.'

'It almost did though. Just a little.'

He ignored her. 'How about the real answer?'

She sighed. 'You know how crazy things are at

work. They'll be that way until the app launches, which is only in a month's time. When I come home after a long day, I can't deal with a messy house. Before I decided to hire Tyler there were dishes in the sink from the weekend. It was Thursday,' she said, dropping her voice, disgusted with herself. 'So, yeah, I called an agency and I got them to send someone to help me.'

Dom took all that in his stride. Or she'd have thought so if she hadn't known him. Since she'd spent many years studying his expressions—and the last five in particular learning what his *My sister's husband is dead so I need to worry about her a million times more* expressions were—she knew he was still concerned.

There hadn't been one day in the year after Kian had died that Dom hadn't worn that concerned expression. In the years after, his expression had vacillated between concern and pretence. She had mostly come out of her depression by then, and he hadn't wanted her to notice his concern and worry. So he'd pretended.

'Dom, it's fine. *I'm* fine.'

'Yeah. Yeah, I know.' He shoved his hands into his pockets. 'So, tell me about this Tyler.'

She shrugged. 'He's a housekeeper.'

'He...?'

She narrowed her eyes. 'Don't be a jerk.'

'I didn't say anything.'

'You didn't have to.'

He smirked. 'So…what? He's been lecturing you on Mochi?'

'He might have witnessed some behavioural things. And I might have expressed some feelings about it.'

'Like the fact that you think your dog adjusting to his new home means he doesn't love you?'

'I did not say that.' *Not in so many words.*

He studied her. 'Okay, sure.' He paused. 'You're okay with this guy?'

'Yeah. I mean, he works for an agency. They vet the people they send out thoroughly. It's the safest way to do this.'

She chose not to tell him Tyler didn't actually work for the agency. Good thing, too, since Dom didn't even seem convinced by the version she had told him. She understood he was worried about her. Understood he'd got Mochi for her because he was worried.

He didn't want her to be alone. As if being alone was some kind of problem that needed to be fixed.

She had thought that, too, in the beginning. Because then being alone had meant she'd had time to think about all the things she and Kian had done. Soon, that progressed to all the things she and Kian had never got to do. Like that trip to Japan he'd always wanted to take. Or building the house they'd always imagined together.

She'd done some of those things as a way to celebrate their union after he was gone. Or had it been a way to grieve? She'd certainly done enough of both during the experiences.

The house had perhaps been the hardest. Still was. Because every day she made tea in the kitchen they'd once dreamed about. She ate at the table they'd been saving to buy in a dining room they'd dreamed of having. She slept in the bedroom they'd designed together and she did it alone. All of it so alone.

The garden was the worst part. Or the best.

But she didn't want to go there right now.

It didn't stop the feeling, the memories, from following her into her home. She resented it, because although it was hard, it was still home. Her comfort. A place for her to relax and dream and reminisce about the past.

But she was used to the ebbs and flow of grief, even years after Kian's death. Perhaps because it was years after death.

When she and Mochi got home, she found Tyler packing containers into the fridge.

Mochi's reaction was somewhere between a yelp and a bark, his excitement apparently too much to contain in a simple response. He ran to Tyler. Brooke was about to tell him not to jump, but Tyler lifted a hand and Mochi skidded to a halt in front of him, almost on his hind legs. But he remained firmly on the ground.

And this is why I don't think he likes me.

She almost said the words out loud, but she didn't want to deal with another conversation about her feelings regarding her dog.

'What are you still doing here?' she asked instead, kicking off her heels—good heavens, how was she still in them?—and throwing her handbag onto the counter. Usually, she discarded both at the front door, but she'd wanted to let Mochi out as soon as possible so he could expend some of his energy in the garden.

'I got caught up making dinner,' he replied, his eyes searching her face as if he could see something worthwhile on it. 'I'll be out of your hair in a couple of minutes.'

'No,' she said quickly. Too quickly for her own liking. 'No, I didn't mean it like that. I just...' She sighed. 'It's been a long day.'

His expression was unreadable. 'Why don't you sit and I'll heat up some food for you?'

'No.'

That answer was as quick as the first. Discomfort turned in her stomach. But feeling the way she felt... She couldn't let this man take care of her in her home.

'Okay,' he said.

'Would you...do you want to go out and get something to eat with me though?' she asked, surprising herself. Because apparently she could let this man comfort her *outside* her home.

'No,' she said, 'please don't answer that. It was inappropriate. I shouldn't have asked. I absolutely don't expect you to have dinner with me. I also don't want you to think that I don't appreciate what you've cooked for me. I'll eat it, I promise. I... I wanted to get out. Which I know sounds weird, since I only got in now, but...'

She trailed off when she realised she was making it worse. She sucked in her bottom lip, then fought for a smile.

'I'm sorry about that, Tyler. Please, feel free to go home. I will see you tomorrow.'

Which she knew was a lie; she would be avoiding him for as long as she possibly could.

'Yes,' he said.

She blinked. 'I'm sorry?'

'Yes. Let's go and get some dinner.'

'But what about the food you made?'

He shrugged. 'It'll keep.'

She thought about it. Well, no, she didn't. She actively didn't think about it. Because she hadn't realised until she'd walked through the front door that she didn't want to be alone. Today, being alone *was* a problem she needed to fix. And if she'd realised that before she'd come home, she would have stayed at Dom's for dinner. Distracted herself.

'You know you don't have to do this, right?' she asked quietly.

His lips curved into a small smile that soothed something inside her. It had the faint sound of alarms going off in her head. But since she wasn't listening to anything going on inside her head, it didn't matter.

'I know,' he said. 'Why don't you take a shower and change, and I'll finish up here?'

She nodded and went upstairs. Her house was all wood and cream, in the design she and Kian had agreed on after the countless vision boards she had forced him to make with her. She adored it, and would have even if Kian hadn't agreed to the design, too. It made going into her bedroom with its soft plush carpet and muted colours more comforting than disarming.

What *was* disarming though, was showering when Tyler was in her house. She put it down to the fact that usually she had her house to herself. She wasn't used to anyone being around. It was as simple as that.

But she was naked, and she couldn't deny that her body was feeling much more than simple. She could see the way her nipples were reacting, her skin turning to gooseflesh, her body aching in places that hadn't ached in literally years.

She turned the water cold so she could blame the reaction of her body on that, and not him. The man who worked for her. The man she hadn't known for more than two days—didn't know anything about, really. The man she'd asked out to dinner.

What am I doing?

She dressed quickly, not answering herself, and went downstairs. Tyler was waiting for her in the living room.

'I put Mochi outside with some food and fresh water.'

'Thank you.' And when that felt awkward, she added, 'Are you sure you want to wear that?' She gestured to the jeans and T-shirt he'd changed into from his suit. 'I happen to know you have a different outfit that would be—'

'Brooke,' he interrupted, his voice gentle but firm. 'Let's go eat.'

And somehow, despite her nerves, she laughed.

It wasn't crossing the line. He was doing what she'd asked. It contravened the distance he'd been determined to put between them, but what should he have done? Said no when she'd looked so... so...*vulnerable*?

He was beginning to realise that look was a trigger. It took him back five years to when he'd thought he was making a new friend. To when he'd thought that their friendship would some-day develop into something more.

He had known at the end of the week, when they'd shared that kiss and she'd all but run from him, that he had been wrong. So why was he act-ing as though this was the first time he'd discov-ered he'd read more into things than he should have? Why was he still trying to find reasons for what had happened?

Like the fact that apparently, she had been married. Or was married. But people who were married lived together, didn't they? Unless their relationship was on the rocks, like his parents' relationship had been before they'd got divorced.

When his father had left to work in Dubai for two years, it had been for the sake of the family. That was what he'd told them. Until two years had become three, then five, and then the end of a marriage.

Back then, his mother had slowly removed all the pictures of his father from the house. His be-longings had followed. Based on that experience, Tyler didn't think Brooke would have a picture of her ex-husband on her fireplace mantel. Ex-cept he hadn't seen any other signs of a man in her home…

He exhaled. He needed to let it go. All of it. The constant memories of the past. The compari-sons. The questions he would get no answers to.

If he was going to survive working for Brooke, he needed boundaries. She had set them by not acknowledging the past, and he'd already decided it wasn't worth it not to respect that. For his sake and Tia's.

Now, he had to set boundaries within himself, too. To remember that everything that had happened was in the past and that he needed to leave it there.

Which he would.

After tonight.

'I know this is pretty far to go for dinner,' Brooke said when they met in the car park. She had taken the lead, with him following her—he tried not to read too much into that—and she'd driven to the beach.

It was a beautiful night for it. The sky was lit with the moon and the stars, as if it were a painting of a perfect night rather than the real thing. The weather was cool, but not cold enough that they needed covering—a welcome reprieve from the heat of the day.

The street was busy, cars and taxis full of people taking advantage of the summer night. From the promenade came the sound of laughter and chattering, of a kind of carefreeness he envied. And beyond the promenade was the beach.

He could only see as far as the night sky allowed, but that was okay. He could hear it. The gentle crash of the ocean, which he knew wouldn't sound so gentle if he went any closer. He could smell the salt in the air, feel the moisture in the breeze when it caressed his face.

'If I'd thought about it, I would have come here, too,' he said.

She took a deep breath. 'I needed it, you know? The ocean and the sound of happiness.'

They lingered, those words, when he didn't reply. But he couldn't manage to. He was caught in the contradiction of her. The way her mouth curved but her eyes glittered with sadness. The relaxed set of her shoulders but the tight way she clasped her handbag.

Despite himself, he remembered the curious mixture of hope and defeat she'd carried with her before, five years ago. It had fascinated him then, too.

He shook it off. 'I'm glad we came.'

She turned to face him, a soft smile eclipsing the confusing emotions on her face. 'That's kind.'

'Don't get used to it,' he said gruffly, when her smile set off an explosion of happy butterflies in his stomach.

His response only had her smile widening.

He braced himself, then said, 'What do you want to eat?'

'Oh, I don't know.' She looked around at the

street, lined with restaurants. 'Should we walk until we find something that appeals to us?'

He nodded and let her lead the way. She chatted casually as they went, pointing out restaurants that looked good or making suggestions. He liked the sound of her voice. She spoke in a unique pattern of rising and falling, as if her words were dancing to some tune only she had the pleasure of hearing. It sounded easier now, as if the tension she'd shown before was slowly escaping from her body like air from a balloon.

It felt as though the tension in him had eased, too.

He shook his head. Did he need to make an appointment with his psychologist? Surely this type of thinking meant he was teetering close to emotional instability?

'What?' she asked.

He looked for Brooke, but she wasn't next to him. She'd stopped walking.

He turned back. 'What?'

'That's what I asked you.'

'Okay. Why did you ask it?'

'You were shaking your head, but I wasn't saying anything.'

'You saw that?'

It was out of his mouth before he could stop it. He'd thought he was too old to blush, but apparently his skin felt differently. It wasn't a light

Oh, this is embarrassing blush either. It was an honest to goodness, *I've spent too much time in the sun* flush.

He cleared his throat. 'I was…thinking.'

She bit her lip, but they both knew she was resisting a smile. 'I would love to ask you what about, but luckily for you I've already crossed too many lines today. I'll let you have your secrets.'

'Thank goodness,' he said on an exhalation. Again, he felt his cheeks heat. His filter seemed to have broken. An annoying development considering he needed it now more than ever. 'What I mean to say is, I don't have any secrets.'

She was no longer resisting the smile now; those lips she'd coated in a whimsical pink were curving in amusement. Heat curved inside him, too. A dangerous heat that was much too close to his heart.

'How about this placc?' she asked, pointing to the restaurant next to them.

'Sure.'

'You didn't even look at it.'

'I'm trying to redirect your attention, and this seemed like a good way to do it.'

She laughed. The sound shot through the air, piercing his chest, turning heat into fire.

'Well, then, let's hope you like it.'

The server seated them at the front of the restaurant, where the doors had been pushed back to the walls, allowing access to both see and hear the ocean. When the woman handed him a menu, he saw that the place specialised in grilled food, which was fortunate. He wasn't sure he could handle anything fancy right now. A good old steak would probably anchor him. Turn his fanciful thoughts and feelings back into parts of himself—*logical* parts of himself—that he could recognise.

Brooke ordered a glass of wine, he ordered a beer, and while they waited she said, 'Again, I'm really sorry I asked you to come to dinner.'

'Why?'

'Well, it's not appropriate.'

'Employees and employers can be friends.'

'Can they?' she asked softly. 'I'm not entirely sure.'

'Is this the first time you've been someone's boss?' he asked.

'No. I…um… I work for a software development company. I'm a lead engineer, so I have a couple of people reporting to me.'

'You're in IT?'

'Yeah.' She tilted her head. 'Why's that surprising to you?'

'It's not.'

A smile played on her lips. 'It very clearly is, Tyler. Is it because I'm a woman?'

'No,' he said quickly. 'Of course not. I believe

women can do anything. If I didn't—which, again, I very much do—my sister and mother would have killed me.'

'They sound like the kind of people I would like.'

His mouth lifted, thinking of it. 'I think they'd like you, too.'

'Yeah? Tell me about them.'

He waited until the server had set their drinks down and they'd placed their dinner orders—steak for both of them—and when she left, Tyler said, 'My mom was a force of nature. She had a couple of jobs. She worked for a call centre during the day and cleaned hotel rooms at night.'

'So housekeeping's in the family?'

'Not sure I'd say that.' He took a moment to figure out how much he wanted to reveal. A lot, as it turned out. 'Tia became a housekeeper after she found out she was pregnant. Things weren't great with the father already, but then she found out he was married.'

Her lips parted, though she didn't respond immediately. 'No wonder you're protective.'

'I'm not… How did you…?'

'Please,' she said, ignoring his splutters. 'You're filling in for her when it's obviously something outside of your area of expertise. I don't mean that you're not doing a good job,' she added quickly. 'I mean because of your actual job. Unless, of course, I'm naïve in believing that you're not a serial killer who's really good at covering your tracks.'

'I'm not a serial killer.' His voice was pained. 'How would I cover my tracks? By creating a full profile of myself online? Establishing an entire business to support that profile?'

'I said you were really good.'

'Brooke, I'm not a criminal.'

'Hmm.'

She reached for her wine and took a deep gulp. She believed him, but Dom's doubts had trickled into her head, forcing her to make sure. Well, it wasn't only Dom's doubts. It was her own. What did she know about this man beyond what he'd told her? Beyond what she'd seen online?

Sure, a man with his online presence and apparent success probably didn't need to trick her into letting him work for her. But how else could she explain the pull she felt towards him? As if they'd shared a past life together, It was giving her the oddest sense of déjà vu.

Surely that was a clue to his ability to manipulate? Manipulation was an important tool for criminals. Never mind that there hadn't been one moment when she'd actually *felt* manipulated.

Apart from that annoying pull, of course.

'Look,' he said after a while. 'I know you have

no reason to trust me, but I'm not lying to you. Yes, I am protective of my sister. She's a single mother, and currently her kid is sick with the chicken pox. I can't look after him, which had been our Plan A, because I've only just got the vaccine and—'

'*What?* Why only now?' she demanded, outraged.

His lips twitched. 'Long story, but I have it now.' He got serious again. 'The point is, Tia has no more leave and she can't afford to lose her job with the agency. She won't let me help her financially,' he said, frustration deepening his voice, 'so this is the only way I *could* help.'

Brooke didn't reply. What could she say? *I believe you, but I need to make sure because I'm attracted to you and I thought I'd lost that part of myself after my husband died.*

It would be selfish. And he obviously was not. The passion when he'd spoken about his family made that clear. He would do anything for them—even step in to do a job with a boss who wouldn't stop interrogating him.

'Would you like to call my sister and check with her?' he asked.

'Yes,' she said, before she could stop herself.

She should have stopped herself.

She didn't want to speak with his sister because she wanted verification, but because she wanted to know more about their relationship. Still, she held out her hand.

'I'd like to speak with her.'

He winced. 'She's going to kill me for this. She'll think I'm risking her job.'

Her hand didn't budge. 'I'll assure her you're doing the opposite. And if that doesn't do it, I'll go to your funeral and pay my respects.'

With an exaggerated sigh—as if he hadn't been the one to suggest it—he tapped his phone screen before handing it to her. Since there weren't many people around them, she put the call on speaker.

'Ty? Where are you? I've been messaging you for ever.'

'Hi, Tia. This is Brooke Jansen. I believe you're supposed to be working for me this month?'

'Ms Jansen?' Tia squeaked. 'Are you…? Hold on…' Tia said, suspicion creeping into her voice. 'Did my brother hire you to trick me?'

'Why would I do that, T?' Tyler inserted.

'Oh, you're there? Lovely,' Tia said, in a tone that indicated she did not find it lovely at all. 'Ms Jansen, I know you have a million reasons to report this to the agency, but I assure you I had no choice. I absolutely wouldn't have done this if Nyle had had anything but the chicken pox.'

'Tia,' Brooke said slowly, 'your brother has

explained the situation to me. I… I understand.'
She caught Tyler's look of relief, but refused to
respond to it. 'I'm just calling to make sure he's
not a criminal. Can you verify?'

'Oh. Well, yeah. He's a dork who runs an online education company.' There was a short pause.
'Wait—you do really believe us? I mean, we could
have coordinated this. I work for the agency, send
my brother in as a replacement, he establishes
some form of trust and if you begin to suspect
something, he has you call me to verify his story.'

'Tia,' Tyler moaned, rubbing a hand on his
forehead. 'What is *wrong* with you?'

'Hey, I'm just looking out for her. She seems
like a nice lady.'

'Thank you,' Brooke said, suppressing a laugh.
'I do believe you. And, while I think going behind the agency's back has some moral problems, you've both dealt with this as ethically as
you could. Besides,' she added wryly, 'I'm pretty
sure that if you two were a criminal duo, one of
you would have ratted the other out by now. Or
you'd both be in prison.'

'Definitely a possibility,' Tia said.

At the same time Tyler said, 'Probably.'

'Not to mention that my brother is a police officer,' Brooke continued conversationally. 'So if
this *is* a ruse, you'll soon be ending your reign
of terror.'

A nervous laugh came through the speaker.

Brooke grinned as she met Tyler's eyes. But he didn't smile back. Just gazed at her with a sincerity and gratitude that made his brown eyes look deeper, more soulful. She hadn't spent much time looking into his eyes—she had some sense of self-preservation—but she wouldn't have said that it was possible. There was enough soul and depth there without any emotion strengthening it. And when emotion did strengthen it…

She exhaled. 'Thank you, Tia. I hope your child feels better soon.'

'Thank you, Ms Jansen—'

'Brooke, please.'

'Thank you, Brooke. I… I appreciate this more than you know.'

After she ended the call, there was a long silence. It wasn't an easy silence either. In fact, she was fairly certain it was filled with cement and steel and everything hard and unyielding. And it sat at the empty seat at their table as if it had been invited to dinner.

Eventually, Tyler cleared his throat. 'Thank you.'

'Don't mention it.'

'I don't mean that casually.' His fingers clenched around his glass of beer. 'Tia's the strongest person I know, but she's stubborn. Proud. We both are.' He swallowed. 'I think if this hadn't worked out she'd have never let me help her again. Not out of stubbornness, but out of fear.'

Brooke understood that better than most.

After Kian had died, she'd felt helpless and so unlike herself. But she'd worked for a company that had thought three weeks' leave was adequate to get her back to who she used to be.

She had trusted those people. Thought they would know that the person she used to be no longer existed.

They hadn't.

When she'd no longer been able to work at the capacity she—and they—were used to, they'd pushed her out. It hadn't been that hard a push; it hadn't needed to be. She had already been perched at the end of a cliff, ready to leave behind everything from the life she'd had with Kian, including her job. She'd only realised afterwards, when she'd been able to work through some of her emotions about the situation, that she'd felt betrayed.

She'd taken a completely different approach when she'd started working for her current company. She didn't trust them, and only saw them for who they were: colleagues and employers. Fear kept her from opening up even a tiny bit in case taking the chance and doing so would leave her in the same position she'd been in at her last company.

So she nodded and said, 'Don't mention it.'

Something in her tone must have told him how much she meant that because he obeyed.

CHAPTER FIVE

'ARE YOU GOING back to your car?' Tyler asked when they'd finished dinner and she'd paid for their meal. She had insisted and, since things hadn't moved away from the confusing and frankly absurd level of awkwardness between them, he'd agreed.

'No, actually. I think I want to take a walk on the beach.'

'I'll come with you.'

'Oh, you don't have to. I would like some time alone, actually.'

'It's after ten p.m.'

Surprised, she glanced at her watch. 'Where did the time go?'

'It's been a long day.'

She curled her fingers over the rim of her bag. 'I should probably get home then.'

He studied her. 'How much do you want to walk on the beach?'

'I don't, really.'

'Brooke.' He waited until she looked at him. 'How much?'

It was a while before she said, 'A lot.'

'Then let's go. You can walk ahead,' he added. 'You'll get your alone time.'

'Well, no. Insisting on that now makes me feel like I'm a terrible person when you're being chivalrous.'

He smiled. 'You can still walk ahead.'

She didn't refuse his offer this time, though she stayed relatively close to him as they crossed the road to the beach. It was much quieter now, only the hardcore night owls strolling down the promenade, making their way to different parts of town where things were livelier.

He took off his shoes when they got there, and he was done before her. Mainly because his shoes didn't have any complicated straps.

'Do you need help?' he asked when she struggled to keep her balance and still couldn't take her shoe off.

'It's fine.'

As she said it, she lost her balance.

Her hands flailed out, trying to find something to steady her. Being the gentleman he was, he became that something.

'This is what I get for being stubborn,' she said, peering up at him.

Because, of course, he hadn't simply offered

her a hand when he'd seen her fall. He'd stepped forward, offering his entire body to stabilise her.

He'd done so without thinking. Truly—it had been instinct. Now he wondered where that instinct came from. Did he really want to help her, or had his body simply wanted to feel hers? He hadn't ever got the chance. Not during that week five years ago. Not until that kiss. And even then, it had only been a meeting of their lips before it ended.

Now here he was holding her. And she was pressed against his chest, as if she were glued there.

She didn't move. At least not her body. Her face was an explosion of movement. Her eyelashes fluttered up at him. Her lips parted. Air, warm and smelling faintly of the mint she'd eaten after dinner, touched his skin. She breathed in deeply, sharply, and exhaled again, hitting him with the warmth of that air again, forcing him to wonder about her taste.

Their kiss hadn't allowed him to sweep his tongue into her mouth and truly *taste* her. Now, she would almost certainly taste like mint. But what about beneath that? His gut told him it would be something sweet, with the slightest hint of a kick.

Except it wasn't his gut. It came from parts of him he hadn't cared about much in the years since he'd met Brooke. Not because he hadn't felt anything for anyone, but because those feelings had seemed inconsequential. Nothing had come close to the spark he'd felt light up his body when his eyes had met Brooke's and lingered.

And this? This felt even better than that spark. Holding her in his arms, feeling her body against his, wondering about something as simple as kissing her.

But nothing about this was simple.

That knowledge had him gently straightening Brooke, ensuring that she had her balance, and taking a step back.

'Thank you,' she said after a moment, her voice shaky.

'Don't mention it.'

It was the same thing she'd said in the restaurant, about the situation with his sister. He'd known she meant it. Now, he hoped she knew he meant it, too.

'Do you mind if I take off your shoes for you?'

'If I say no, that would make me a fool, wouldn't it?' she teased.

Teased. As if she hadn't felt her world shift only seconds ago, as he had. But he could pretend to be unaffected, too.

'Are you a fool?' he asked mildly.

'I'm sure the answer to that changes in each situation, but for this one? No.'

He was smiling as he lowered himself to the ground to take off her shoes. He wasn't sure why. It seemed his emotions were on a cross-country ride, going from panic and desire to amusement and calm in too little time for him to process.

Though the strap of one shoe was already undone, she hadn't managed to actually take off the shoe. He did that, then started on the next.

Seconds into the task, she leaned closer to him, resting her hand on his shoulder. Before that, he had been able to pretend that her proximity wasn't affecting him. He couldn't any more. He felt electrocuted, and he was grateful for the dark so she couldn't see his hands shaking.

Desire covered his skin as if it were in the breeze that passed them. But he refused its call. Refused to allow himself to feel as though he were a teenage boy unable to handle his hormones.

When he straightened and she smiled and thanked him, he felt very much like that teenage boy. Zero to one hundred in a matter of seconds, and then all the way back again.

'Are you okay?' she asked, frowning.

'Yeah,' he said, his voice hoarse. He cleared his throat. 'Yes. Why?'

'You seem…strange.'

'That hardly seems like the kind of thing you should say to someone who's helped you.'

'That's probably true. Although we've already established that I'm not good at saying what I'm supposed to say when I'm supposed to say it.'

'What do you mean?'

'I asked you to come out for dinner with me even though you work for me.'

'I thought we'd already settled that?'

'We have,' she agreed. 'I'm just pointing out that there are some flaws in my being.'

He laughed softly, though he wasn't sure why.

'But now that the truth's out am I really your boss?' she asked. 'Technically, your sister's my employee.'

'Does that mean I don't have to do the job then?'

'Huh,' she said. 'Good point. We should probably still work within the confines of an employer/employee relationship.'

He was certain she didn't mean that in the way he took it, but he couldn't help but agree. It was best if they stayed as boss and employee. Sure, she was right: it wasn't the traditional relationship. But for the sake of his sanity, he would cling to it.

'Sounds good to me,' he replied.

'I thought it might.'

Her words hung in the air between them as they walked in silence.

* * *

There were no more impromptu dinner requests, no more inappropriate comments, and certainly no more touching after that night. Brooke made sure of it.

Except she did it in the only way she knew how: she avoided being at home.

She left before Tyler arrived and came back late enough that if he was still there, she would warn him about working too hard. Fortunately, she had enough work to warrant the long hours. Her latest project was going well, but she still had a lot to do before the app launched in three weeks. So Brooke kept busy.

Still, she couldn't get Tyler out of her mind. Mainly because he kept doing stuff for her that made her think about him.

A few nights after their dinner, she came home to a note.

Walked Mochi today. Twice. He's the kind of dog who needs it. Might be useful to know for the future.
Tyler

She was relieved. At first. But when she thought about it, she felt only guilt. Because she was Mochi's owner; he was *her* responsibility. And it wasn't because she needed to work that she was neglecting him. She was doing it because she didn't want to see Tyler.

So the next day she took Mochi for a walk before she left for work and left Tyler a note of her own.

Walked Mochi before I went to work. I can do it again later, so you don't have to. He's not your responsibility.
Brooke

She was already at work when she thought back to the note and wondered if it sounded defensive. And as soon as that occurred to her, she couldn't get it out of her head. More than once, one of her employees checked to see if she was okay.

She did not appreciate it. Nor did she appreciate Tyler's note when she got home.

Walked Mochi this evening so you don't have to. Also put a lasagne in the fridge. You can freeze the rest when you're done.
Tyler

PS I'm here to help you with your responsibilities. That's exactly what you're paying me—well, Tia—to do.

She was so annoyed that she almost refused to eat the food. But she had nothing ready-made in the fridge, and calling out to get food would take too long. She was hungry, and cooking wasn't an option—when was it ever?—so she dished up a portion of the lasagne.

It was the best thing she'd eaten.

Damn it.

'Why does he keep doing this?' she asked Mochi as she lifted a forkful of lasagne from her second helping. 'I don't want him to be nice. I would honestly prefer him to be a complete and utter jerk who isn't competent at his job.'

And he was more than competent; her house was in a better state than she could ever make it herself.

'Hell, I'll take the aloof and distant guy he was when we met. Except even then he was thoughtful. He made me food that very first night! And now he makes the best lasagne in the world! The cheek!'

Mochi tilted his head, as if to say, *I don't see the problem here.*

'Is this why you like him? Because he's nice?'

Mochi didn't answer.

'Well, it won't work on me.'

She finished her meal, washed the dishes, then went to the garden to play catch with Mochi for a little while before bed.

As it usually did, the garden calmed her. It was the first thing she had done in the house. The space had been the reason she'd bought it after all.

When they'd started dating, Kian had told her they would get married someday. It had been a ridiculous thing to say at the start of a relationship, but they'd been young and he'd been her first boyfriend. And sure, the fact that her parents had met and fallen in love almost instantly had had some effect on her. They were the happiest couple she knew—of course it would affect her. So she hadn't run away, as her instinct now would be, from a silly man and his silly romantic proclamation.

For her birthday that year, Kian had given her a framed landscape design.

'For our home,' he'd said, 'when we're married.'

He had still been studying back then, but his talent had been evident. He'd died before the world could truly take advantage of that talent, which had made his gift so much more meaningful. She was one of the few people who had an original Kian Jansen design. It would have seemed almost rude not to follow through.

It had taken years after his death, but she'd done it, and she was proud.

Though it might not be the best garden for a

dog, she thought, as she accidentally threw the ball into the pond and Mochi jumped in after it.

He brought the ball back to her with a wagging tail and a drenched body.

She heaved out a sigh. 'We probably need to sort you out now, don't we?'

She left him outside when she went to fetch his leash. She was about to go back out when the doorbell rang. Wondering who it could be, so late, she peeked through the eyehole and saw Tyler.

It took her a couple of minutes—and another ring of the bell—to answer.

'Tyler?' she said, acting surprised. She probably wouldn't win any awards for it. 'What are you doing here? It's almost nine p.m.'

'I left my wallet here.'

He shoved his hands into his pockets. The movement made his muscles ripple. Not that she noticed.

'Can I get it?'

'Sure.' She opened the door wider.

'Thanks.' A second later, he asked, 'Where's Mochi?'

'Outside,' she said with a sigh. 'There was an accident.'

'Are you okay?'

'Yeah, we're fine. We were playing and I threw the ball in the pond and he went to get it. So…'

she lifted the leash '...we're going to have a bath before bed.'

'That sounds like an exciting way to end a long day of work.'

She snorted. 'Exactly!'

'I can help,' he said. She noticed the words came tentatively. 'If you want.'

'Oh, no. It's fine. I mean, I was just going to bring him into the bathroom...'

'Wet?'

She hadn't thought about that. 'Well, I don't know if I can do it in the garden. A couple of the outside lights aren't working and I forgot to buy bulbs to replace them—'

'And you didn't think to ask your house-keeper?'

She paused. 'That does sound like something I should have done, doesn't it?'

He watched her for a moment, then said, 'Brooke, you hired me because you needed help. So why don't you want me to help you?'

Because I've been thinking about the way you held me on the beach every day since. Because I can remember the heat of your touch, the strength of your body. Because you're the kind of man who helps his sister out but does it in the least dishonest way possible. Because you helped me take off my shoes, even when I was too stubborn to ask you at first. Because you walked with

*me on the beach after, and you walked my dog,
and all of it feels like asking you to help would
be more intimate than I can stand right now.*

'I'm not used to help,' she said honestly, because she was still processing all the other
stuff—she hadn't expected her brain to be quite
so honest at this time of night—and she didn't
particularly want to process it.

'You hired me.'

'Because I need help. Which, yes, I know
makes me seem stupid for not asking for it, but…
but it's a habit, okay? I had to learn how to rely
on myself and now it's a habit. I didn't have to
for the longest time. First, my parents did everything for me. Then Kian. And when he died, I—'

She broke off at the expression on his face. Re-
played everything she said. When she realised
she'd spoken about Kian, her face heated.

It wasn't because she was embarrassed to talk
about him. It was more that she hadn't realised
she *had* talked about him. And sharing his name
or her experiences before and after his death,
didn't feel like something she should be sharing
with Tyler. Again, it felt too intimate.

'Kian?' Tyler prodded softly.

Of course he did.

And what other choice did she have but to tell
him?

'My husband. He died five years ago.'

* * *

Tyler's mind spun with this new information. He hadn't thought he would hear anything like it from Brooke. She had closed up on him since that day at the beach. Not that she had been an open book that night, but she had been easier than this. He had known it even though he hadn't seen her since the beach. And it was part of the reason he'd doubled back this evening.

Oh, he'd definitely forgotten his wallet. But he could have easily collected it the next day. When he convinced himself to go round at nine p.m., he wondered if his subconscious hadn't been the thing to make him leave his wallet behind. He wanted to check on her, make sure she was okay. Perhaps see whether she was still as affected by their night at the beach as he was.

Her notes seemed to indicate otherwise, but it was entirely possible that she was deflecting her feelings—or that he was grasping at literally anything to make the fact that he couldn't stop thinking about her, his possibly married boss, less alarming.

But she wasn't married. She was a widow. Had been for five years. Which might have made his pining a little less creepy if it hadn't caused other questions about the time they'd spent together five years ago.

Had she been married then? Had her husband

already passed away? If so, how long before they'd met? And did that change anything?

He couldn't answer those questions without speaking to her, but since she seemed determined to forget that they'd even met before, he couldn't exactly ask her.

Unless he should.

Should he?

No. He was leaving the past behind him. Boundaries and all that.

With a shallow breath, he said, 'I'm incredibly sorry to hear that.'

She lifted her shoulders, a gesture meant to indicate that it wasn't a big deal but one that only succeeded in telling him it was a very big deal.

'It's been five years. I'm okay with it for the most part.'

'But it lingers, doesn't it?'

She looked at him, blinked. And with that blink, something cleared in her vision. 'You've lost someone, too.'

It wasn't a question, but he replied. 'My mother.'

'I'm sorry,' she murmured. 'When you spoke about her the other night…' She trailed off, as if she'd just realised he'd spoken about his mother in the past tense. 'I should have realised.'

Three sharp barks came from the garden.

Brooke winced. 'Clearly he'd like us to have this conversation some other time.'

Since it would give him the break he needed to gather his thoughts, Tyler nodded. 'Do you have a bucket or something to wash him in?'

'I do. It's in the garage. Should we bring him inside? The light out there is bad.'

'I'm sure we can manage between the two of us.'

She nodded. 'Let's do it.'

She gave him instructions on where she kept the dog shampoo and an old towel. Minutes later, Tyler was running water into the bucket in the downstairs bathroom. When it was done, he carried it outside, to where Mochi and Brooke were waiting.

Brooke was murmuring comfort to the dog as he laid his head on her knee. It hit Tyler in an entirely unexpected way. Not only the intimacy of the moment, but the desire for it to be...permanent. Because of it, water splashed over the rim of the bucket before he could put it down.

'That's what you get for showing off,' she said tartly, but she smiled before uncurling her legs and standing.

What was it about this woman that he couldn't stop himself from being drawn to her? He wanted to know things about her he shouldn't want to know. Like the way she'd become independent after years of not being. How had that affected her? Was that the reason she couldn't see how deeply her dog loved her? Was that why she berated herself for not having the boundaries she thought she should have with him?

But why did he care about any of it? She had a husband. She'd *had* a husband when they'd met or she had just lost her husband. Either way, the situation was a minefield he shouldn't want to navigate.

He knew all about relationship minefields. His parents' relationship… Tia's relationship with Nyle's father… They'd both shown him how complicated things could be. And they hadn't had the added factor of a dead spouse who might have been alive when they'd first met.

'You okay?' she asked, studying him now as she held Mochi while he shampooed the dog.

'Why wouldn't I be?' He offered her a smile that he was certain wouldn't reassure her. He was right.

'You're awfully quiet. Did I bruise your ego earlier?' she teased.

Damn if his heart didn't skip at the easiness. At the longing for it to be easy, only easy, between them.

'My ego is fine.'

'Your feelings then.' Her tone shifted to something more serious. 'You're upset that I was making fun. I didn't mean—'

'I'm fine, Brooke,' he interrupted curtly, and immediately regretted it.

Hurt skipped across her face, but it was gone so quickly. 'Of course.'

They washed Mochi in silence for the next few moments. The dog whined softly, though he didn't try to move. Tyler wondered if that meant he wasn't whining at being bathed, but at the tension between the humans who were bathing him.

When they were done, Brooke said, 'I can take it from here.'

'What?'

'I have the leash and his brush, and it won't take any longer or be any easier with you around.' She winced, as if she regretted the phrasing, but she didn't correct herself. 'You can get your wallet and go. I'm sure you have other places to be.'

'Brooke—'

'I can do this by myself, Tyler,' she said, more sternly now.

What could he say to that?

He nodded, stood up, grimacing at the sight of his own clothing that was wet in patches now. But he didn't say anything. Only dusted his feet off as best he could, grabbed his wallet and went to his car.

Once there, he hit the edge of the steering wheel. 'Idiot!'

Because he was and he deserved to hear it. Any progress they'd made tonight—and he felt as if they'd made some—had been completely and utterly ruined because he couldn't get out of his own head.

It was probably for the best that she'd kicked him out. There was no telling how much more damage he would have done if he'd stayed.

CHAPTER SIX

BROOKE SUCCESSFULLY PUSHED Tyler out of her head until Friday.

She was quite proud of herself, honestly. She hadn't thought about him, or the way she could almost still feel his skin on hers from that night on the beach, or the way he wanted to help her and then didn't. Or maybe he did, but there was something that had kept him from being comfortable that night with Mochi.

She didn't have much experience, but she couldn't imagine knowing that she was a widow made things easy. Not that it was some thing to be made easy when there was nothing going on between them. It wasn't like they were starting a relationship and he was freaked out by the fact that she had once been married and the only reason she wasn't now was because her husband had died.

But, since she wasn't thinking about it, it didn't matter anyway. And that was why she was almost okay when she walked into her kitchen that morning to find him sitting at the counter with his laptop open.

'Morning,' she said, going to the coffee machine.

He'd already made it, which wasn't a thoughtful thing she needed to get mushy about. It was his *job*. He was doing his job, not thinking about her.

It was the same thing every time he made her food.

Bought her groceries.

Discovered what her favourite scent was and put candles in her study and her bathroom.

Fluffed her pillows and made them smell like that same scent.

Left notes when he'd walked Mochi.

All of it was his job.

All of it.

She gulped down her coffee, not even caring that it burnt her throat.

'Rough night?' he asked, watching her.

Determination alone couldn't stop her from blushing, so she just said, 'Yeah. We've been testing an app that's launching soon. There have been some bugs, but nothing hectic. I can't imagine that'll continue, so I'm trying to prepare myself.' The blush got deeper when she realised he probably hadn't wanted to know any of that. 'Everything okay with you?'

She was looking at him properly now, so she could see the faint shadows under his eyes.

'Of course.'

'You said that a little too quickly.'

He offered her a wry smile. And instantly she knew she would no longer be able to resist thinking about him. Because of that smile.

His eyes softened, the skin around them crinkled as his cheeks lifted. The curve of his mouth thinned his lips, though that didn't lessen the seductive quality of them one bit. Hell, if anything, it made her want to lean in and—

She froze. She found him attractive, yes, but that attraction had never taken a detour into fantasy. She wasn't sure how she should feel about it.

But worrying about that was for another time. Now was for worrying about something else: those shadows under his eyes.

'You're more perceptive than most people,' he said.

'Maybe. Doesn't change the fact that you said it too quickly.'

He exhaled, as if in defeat. She would have enjoyed it more if he hadn't looked so... Well, defeated.

'What is it, Tyler?' she asked, her heart picking up on his tension and beating faster than she liked. 'Please, for heaven's sake, don't keep me in suspense.'

He sighed, but he answered. 'My company…
has been offered an opportunity to expand.'

'Okay?'

'From a company in the UK,' he continued
after a beat. 'It would mean… Well, it would
mean that I'd have to live there for a while, and
I can't do that.'

'Why not?'

'I'm the only family Tia and Nyle have. I can't
abandon them.'

She opened her mouth to point out that it
wouldn't be abandoning them, but the conflict
in his eyes stopped her. A simple observation
wouldn't do him any good when he was in this
state. Especially since him even using the word
'abandon' meant he must have had some baggage.

Instead, she said, 'So what's with the sad eyes
on your laptop now?'

'The company is trying to tempt me.'

She searched his face. 'And it's working.'

'No,' he answered, though it hadn't been a
question. 'No, it's not.'

'Tyler—'

'Does my attending one of their events over
here tonight sound like a good idea? Maybe,'
he said, as if she hadn't spoken. 'I'd learn more
about the company, the people I'd potentially be
working with. I could engage with them on my
ideas about how the expansion would work…'

If he hadn't seemed so torn up about it, she would have told him to stop drooling.

'But,' he went on, 'that would only be relevant *if* I were interested.'

'Which you are.'

'No.'

She waited to see if there was more, then said, 'Tyler, you're interested. There's nothing wrong with that. You haven't betrayed anyone by being interested.' When he didn't say anything, she prodded. 'That's it, right? You think you're betraying your family?'

'I think…' It was a while before he finished the sentence. 'Yeah, I do. Being interested is the first step towards doing something, isn't it?'

It was a rhetorical question, but somehow she felt as though she needed to answer. Perhaps because it resonated with her, and unknowingly, it pointed out one of her own issues. She was interested in Tyler. And, yes, that did feel as though she was moving towards betraying Kian.

She didn't need her therapist to tell her that it was a normal part of moving forward. They'd spoken about it plenty of times with regard to other areas of her life. Her work, her home. Even her family. Whenever her life changed or evolved she felt guilty because it was changing and evolving away from the life she'd shared with Kian.

At the same time she felt as if she had to move forward. She owed it to him.

But did she owe it to him to move on with *this* part of her life?

'It's complicated,' she answered softly.

'Yes.' He paused. 'I haven't told my sister.'

'Okay.'

'I told myself I would mention it in passing,' he said. 'So that I could get her opinion on it. I was hoping...'

When he didn't finish, she finished for him. 'That she'd give you the permission you feel you need from her to do something you really want to do.'

He opened his mouth—to argue, she thought, seeing his body tense. But he deflated quickly. 'Yes.'

'And you haven't told her because...?'

'Because I'm a coward.'

'That doesn't sound fair,' she chided.

He gave her a sad look. A defeated look. It crashed into her heart as if it were a car going too fast on a highway. And, just like that car, she had apparently lost control, too, because she found herself saying, 'What if I went with you?'

His eyes widened. That was his only reaction. He didn't respond verbally, didn't move a muscle beyond that. And when, after at least a million minutes of silence, he still didn't reply, Brooke set her half-full mug on the counter and wiped her palms—sweaty now—on her trousers.

'Well, that's all the time I have this morning,' she said, knowing she sounded like a talk show host. 'I guess I'll see you around.'

But probably not.

Then she basically sprinted from the kitchen. The scene of her death.

Fortunately, when she got to work there was an urgent issue that kept her from thinking about anything that had happened that morning. But by lunchtime things had quietened and mortification filled her.

'Why did I think that would be a good idea?' she asked out loud, squeezing her stress ball with its smiley face for all it was worth. 'I'm not ready for it to be a date, but that's what I offered, right? Or was I offering something a friend would do? Except we're not friends, so now it's...' She trailed off. 'Now it's confusing. For both of us.'

She sighed. Blamed it on his expression. That look of hopelessness and frustration and defeat. She wanted to get his smile back. It was somehow imprinted on her brain, regardless of how much she wanted it not to be. Especially when she could barely remember Kian's face these days...

Most of the time, she understood. This was what happened. Those vivid memories of every detail of his face, his body, had faded over time. She remembered the general things about Kian, and that was what was most important.

He had been handsome in such a traditional sense of the word that when she'd been with him, she'd often tell him how annoying it was. He had been strong, but not in any way dictated by the gym. His strength had come from the time he'd spent outdoors. Hiking or running or carrying things when he was messing around in a garden. And he had been kind. So kind that some days she had marvelled at him. Tried to be more like him. And, really, those *were* the most important things.

But it smarted, just a little, that she could remember everything about Tyler. The light in his eyes when he smiled at her unexpectedly; the curve of his lips that courted his cheeks; the scar he had next to his right eye that was hardly noticeable to someone who wasn't determined to notice everything about him.

He wasn't traditionally handsome. No, his features were too rugged, too sharp for that. But there was something about the way they came together. Or maybe it was the way he carried himself. With a confidence that told her he didn't care about being handsome. With the easiness of not caring.

It was clear he cared about other stuff though.

His family was important to him. There was obviously more to the situation than she knew, but
she could understand his concerns about going
overseas. She couldn't imagine leaving the only
family she had or having them leave her. If she
had to choose between that and moving forward
with her life? That decision wouldn't be easy.

A glance at the clock told her lunchtime was
over and she got back to work. But no matter how
hard she tried, Tyler crept into her consciousness.
She was immensely relieved when she got home
that evening and discovered she was alone.

But when she walked into the kitchen, she
found a note on the fridge.

*I'd like to take you up on your offer. Please.
You'll find what you need in your bedroom.
I'll be over at seven.
T*

'This is a joke, right?' she asked the empty
room.

For a full five seconds she expected an answer. Someone to jump out of the closet and say,
How did you figure it out? and then she wouldn't
have to go to her bedroom and find out what he
thought she needed.

She looked at the clock. It was almost six. She
had an hour to figure out what to wear, to do

her hair, her make-up. And she hadn't done anything of the sort in years. An hour was not what she would have given herself to rediscover those skills.

'Okay. Okay,' she said because apparently today, speaking out loud was the only thing keeping her from panicking. 'One thing at a time.'

She got Mochi's food ready, went out to feed him, then refilled his water and gave him some belly rubs with the promise of a long morning walk. Then she went to her bedroom.

There was a gold dress hanging on her cupboard.

Something strange happened to her breathing. She inhaled sharply, exhaled, then exhaled again, as if somehow she had more than enough air in her lungs. Slowly she moved forward, touched the material. It was silk...smooth. It felt like luxury. She dropped it, worried that she would damage it somehow by simply touching it.

On the floor beneath the dress was a shoe box. She almost didn't open it, afraid of what extravagance she would find there. But she dropped down, opened the lid. She was more prepared this time, but it still felt like an out-of-body experience. The shoes were gold perfection, their straps covered with shiny stones that she traced and immediately loved.

She straightened, shook her head. She couldn't

malfunction right now, no matter how much she wanted to. She needed to get her hair done, which would likely take most of her time. And then she needed to figure out make-up; she couldn't remember what the appropriate style was.

With a deep breath, she started preparing.

CHAPTER SEVEN

HE WAS HOLDING his breath. It was a stupid thing to do, considering he needed air to survive. But as he rang Brooke's doorbell—it would have felt like an invasion to walk in—he held his breath.

Tyler wished he had dealt with the situation differently that morning. When she'd offered, he wished he hadn't frozen. Why hadn't he accepted her kindness then? It would have made it less awkward, especially when she was doing something for him.

But, no—he *had* frozen. He had frozen because he'd wanted to say yes so quickly he'd been afraid of what it might tell her if he did. He also hadn't expected it. He'd been so in his own mind, berating himself for not being honest with Tia, for wanting things he couldn't have, for admitting all that to a woman he felt so complicatedly about, that her offer had come out of left field. By the time his mouth had caught up, she'd been out the house.

The least he could do then was get her attire

sorted so things were as easy for her as possible. Hopefully it would help so she wouldn't regret her decision.

Although he was fairly certain it was too late for that.

The door opened before he could think on it for too long. And then he wasn't thinking at all.

'I think it might be a size too small,' Brooke said, instead of greeting him.

That was fine with him. Because the fact that she'd said it meant he could look at her without it seeming as if he was ogling.

Though he absolutely was.

The dress was sleeveless, revealing firm brown arms. One strap was thin, widening into gold material that clung to her breast in a teardrop shape, while the other strap was thicker, falling into loose fabric that covered the rest of her chest and then cinched in at the waist. From there, the dress flowed to the ground, sweeping over shoes that looked beautiful on her feet.

'You look incredible.' Quickly he realised she might not be comfortable with the dress. 'I'm sorry. I should have checked with you.'

'No, no, it's okay.'

Her fingers tightened around the clutch purse he'd bought. Gold as well, though simpler than the dress.

'I was just worried that this area—' she made

a circle above her chest '—would be distracting.' She changed the subject abruptly. 'I didn't realise this event would be so formal.'

'It's a cocktail party. Hence the suit and the dress.'

'You…um…you look nice too.'

'Thank you.' He paused. 'Do you feel uncomfortable?'

She shifted. 'Not about the dress.' She winced. 'I didn't mean that the way it sounded.'

'It's okay,' he said. 'I get it. I feel it, too. The only reason I got dressed and decided to go through with this is because you offered to come with me. I'm not… I'm still not sure I want to do this.'

She reached out to take his hand. 'You want to do this.'

His throat felt odd for a moment, but he swallowed and the moment passed. 'Thank you. Thank you for coming tonight.'

'Don't mention it.'

She dropped his hand, curved her fingers around her ear as though there was hair there. But she had sleeked her hair back, curled her edges in a fascinating pattern over her forehead. The rest of it fell in a long, straight ponytail down her back.

It made her face stand out all the more, though he had no idea how that was possible. She already had the most striking features he'd encountered. But without any hair framing her face he could see the smoothness of her brown skin, the little dots on her cheeks, the full, plump lips, the dark, thick lashes. All of those features were more prominent because she'd put on make-up. Black encircled her eyes, a light pink touched her cheeks, a deep red coloured her lips.

Her breasts weren't the distraction he was worried about; *she* was. By simply being at his side. Of course it didn't help that she looked like a goddess on a day designated to celebrate her greatness. He was willing to bet she'd distract everyone in the room tonight.

That might not be such a bad thing. He might not feel as much pressure about being there if she did.

'Is it strange that I'm nervous?' she asked, stepping out of the house and locking up behind her. 'I'm only the plus one.'

You could never only be the plus one, he wanted to say. Thank heavens he stopped himself. 'Maybe you're feeding off my nerves,' he said instead.

He held out his hand, offering her support if she wanted it. Her eyes dropped, lingered, then she took it.

'It'll be fine,' she said, to both of them.

He swore he heard her voice shake, but he couldn't be sure.

He didn't react at the contact as he helped her down the stairs to his car. But holding her hand felt as though he was holding something precious. He couldn't drop it, no matter what.

He opened the passenger door before going to the driver's side and getting in himself.

'What should I know?' she asked as he drove down the short path from her house to her gate. 'About this event?'

He told her what he knew about the company and its possible areas of expansion. When that led to questions about his own work, he answered them. Explained how his mother hadn't been able to study when she was younger because she hadn't been given the opportunity to do so. And how when the opportunity had come—when her family life and financial position had finally aligned to allow it—his father left.

'She was essentially a single parent,' he said, trying to keep the emotion out of his voice. 'And her dreams got delayed even longer.'

'Why did your father leave?' Brooke asked softly.

He hesitated. It wasn't because the information was a secret, but because sharing it with her felt... It felt like crossing a line again. One of his own lines this time. One of those boundaries he'd told himself he had to keep when he'd started working for her.

But then, almost as soon as he'd set them those lines had become blurred. He knew it simply because the distance he'd planned to treat her with had slowly but surely disappeared. He couldn't be cool with her, despite their history. Despite the fact that that history was apparently more complicated than he'd originally thought.

They were edging into new territory, and he had no idea how to handle it.

In this case she saved him from deciding as she said, 'Since your thinking is steaming up the car—which, as I say it, sounds like a dangerous way of phrasing it—I'll change the subject.' She pivoted, exactly as she said she would. 'So, you're basically saying that you started your company to provide online learning specifically geared towards people of an older generation, who have a lot on their plates, because you were thinking of your mother?'

'Yes,' he answered, both relieved and oddly disappointed. 'I had been looking into different programmes for her to follow when I realised that with her schedule, she wouldn't be able to fit much in. I thought I'd try to design something bespoke for her, and as I was doing that, I thought it might actually work for more people than her.'

He took the turn-off for the highway, saw Table Mountain in the distance. If he didn't take this opportunity—and he wouldn't—at least he would still have this. His home. His memories.

The beauty of Cape Town was so inextricably linked with those memories that he'd never give it up. He couldn't. Not when Tia still needed him. Not when his mother wouldn't have wanted him to. She had made so many sacrifices for them. For their happiness. To ensure that they still felt like a unit, a family, after his father left. She would be ashamed of him for even considering taking the same path as his father.

'There you go, thinking again.'

He exhaled. 'I'm sorry. It—*this*—is harder than I thought it would be.'

'What is?'

'Thinking about what I want. Tia and I weren't raised that way. We were raised to think about family. My father left and it was the three of us and… Well, we had to be there for one another.'

'You can still be there for your family if you do this, Tyler,' she pointed out. 'You're not disappearing off the ends of the earth. You're taking an opportunity that will—what? Require you to spend some time in a different country? That's not abandoning by any means.'

'My father took an opportunity that required him to spend some time in a different country,' he said quietly. 'A job in Dubai. He was doing okay here, but he wanted us to be more comfortable, he said. So he left.' He took a steadying breath. 'A two-year contract turned into a permanent situation. He started a brand-new life without us and we had to accept it.'

'I'm sorry,' she murmured, the words heavy despite her soft tone.

Silence followed, and he realised he was supposed to fill it. He shrugged. 'Now you know why this isn't simple.'

'Yeah.' There was a long pause again. 'I get it. I mean, I know how hard it is to move forward when something in your past keeps pulling you back.' She gave a light snort. 'Even saying it that way sounds bad. Like my dead husband is a hindrance of some kind.' She exhaled. 'Sorry. That was morbid.'

'No,' he said, taking her hand. 'It was honest.'

She nodded, looking out of the window. 'Anyway, my point is that I do get it. I feel the guilt and the betrayal and the resentment, too. It sounds like yours is directed at your father, which is fair. Mine… Mine is directed at me. Because how can I be angry at someone for dying?'

She shook her head. Opened her mouth. Before she could utter the apology he was sure she intended, he squeezed her hand.

'Don't,' he told her. 'Don't feel bad for sharing. That's how you feel and it's honest. There's no shame in that.'

'I… Thank you.'

He nodded. Let the silence linger until he pulled into a parking space and said, 'I guess I'll be doing this for both of us. Taking a small step forward.'

She blinked, but her lips slowly curved into a smile. 'I like that. I like that very much.'

Brooke walked out of the elevator slowly, appropriately impressed by what she saw.

There was the mountain, of course. The layout had been angled so that most of the room faced it, but she was more enamoured by the view of the city.

It was busy, as to be expected on a Friday night. The sound of traffic fluttered up, occasionally interrupted by the sound of human beings living: laughing and talking and an infrequent shriek. It reminded her of that night at the beach, multiplied by a thousand.

Because that was what the centre of Cape Town was. The sound of life times a thousand. That was what she loved about it.

The venue was beautiful. The rooftop was lit with classy light bulbs, strung across the space as though they were stars. She looked to see how they were being held up, but the poles weren't obvious. The bar was on one side, and a dessert station was next to it, but apparently the main course would be plated.

'It's an odd decision to have dessert there,' she said, tilting her head as she stared at a chocolate fountain. 'What about people who have no self-control? Or who prefer to have dessert before dinner?'

'Where do you fall?' Tyler asked, grabbing two flutes of champagne and handing her one.

'Why do I have to choose?'

She smiled. When he smiled back, she realised it wasn't her smartest decision. Because he had an effect on her. The entire package of him in that suit, its black lines skimming his impressive shoulders, the shirt beneath it clinging to a chest she wished she knew more about it. And when he smiled, with that crinkling of his eyes...

She felt as if she was the only person in the world.

She had no right to feel that way. Especially when they'd just spoken about how difficult it was to move on. Because she knew it, she downed her flute of champagne, wishing she could be as light as one of those bubbles. Floating away into the night sky, avoiding all her desires.

'We should probably speak to people, right?' she asked.

'Right.' He took her empty glass, replaced it with a full one as if it didn't concern him at all that hers was empty when he'd barely touched his. 'Let's go find some people.'

People loved him. Of course they did. He was easy and charming and he smiled. A lot. And not in a creepy way, but in a way that made people feel comfortable. The British company was clearly courting him. Each conversation was a pitch hidden in mundane observation. She could sense their respect in all of it. She wondered if he realised how much they wanted him.

He introduced her as his 'friend,' which didn't feel like the right description. But then, she didn't know what the right description would be. If they weren't friends, and they weren't in a relationship, what was left? Employer and employee? And since neither of them wanted to explain *that* situation, friend seemed like the safest bet.

For dinner, they were seated at a long table in the middle of the room, with the CEO of the company that was courting Tyler and a few more executives. It wasn't as bad as she expected, making conversation with strangers. She hadn't done it in a long time, but that didn't mean she couldn't do it.

The knowledge subtly nudged something inside her. It took her a moment to realise it was her confidence. She hadn't been avoiding social situations because she didn't have the skills to navigate them. She'd been doing it because she hadn't been ready to face them. And now... Well, now she thought that maybe she was.

At the end of the dinner, music began to play and some people moved to the dance floor. Others went to the bar.

She went to get dessert.

'You've been waiting all evening for this, haven't you?' Tyler asked when she told him.

'Why would you say that?' she asked innocently, but winked. 'Should I get you anything?'

His lips had parted and he was staring at her. For a short moment, she thought he might be having some kind of medical episode.

'Tyler...?'

'Sorry.' He blinked. 'Get me whatever you're getting.'

'I'm not sure you can eat all I'm getting.'

He smiled, but still seemed distracted. 'Try me.'

'If you insist.'

She grabbed a tray and began putting two of everything that appealed to her on a plate. She was reaching for an eclair when someone started speaking.

'You're Brooke, right? You're here with Tyler?'

'What?'

She turned, found herself staring at a woman with long dark hair. Brooke hadn't spoken to her yet that evening; she was the spouse of one of the executives who had been sitting some distance away from them.

'You're Tyler Murphy's wife?'

She opened her mouth, exhaled a little, then managed a smile. 'No. We're…we're friends.'

'Oh. I'm sorry. You both…' She shook her head, a blush lighting her cheeks.

She hadn't said it to get a reaction, Brooke realised. She'd genuinely thought Brooke and Tyler were married.

'We both what?'

'I've already made this more uncomfortable than it needed to be. I shouldn't have assumed.'

'I'd like to know,' Brooke said softly, though she was almost certain she didn't.

'You both look…close.' She lifted a shoulder. 'Like you have a secret no one else is privy to. That's how people used to describe me and my husband. But I've clearly made a mistake.' She offered a tentative smile. 'Friends can have that, too.'

Except she and Tyler weren't really friends.

She was right; she hadn't wanted the answer at all.

CHAPTER EIGHT

Since Brooke had come back with their dessert, she'd been acting strangely.

Of course, it could have been a reaction to the way he'd malfunctioned when she'd winked at him. His body had simply gone haywire. It had taken one teasing wink, reimagined in an entirely different context—something much more intimate than a formal function—and suddenly he'd been hotter than the evening called for and immensely glad his lower body was obscured by a table.

But it couldn't be that. Brooke hadn't seemed to notice the moment, and he didn't want to project when the reason for her behaviour could be entirely different.

A slow song began to play. More people moved to the dance floor, and he thought he might have a chance to figure it out.

'Would you like to dance?'

Brooke's hand paused as it brought a spoonful of chocolate mousse to her mouth. 'Now?'

'After that bite, if you'd like.'

She blushed, but despite that, her hand hovered, as if she were deciding what the best course of action might be. He started to hide his smile—but what was the point? So he watched her, enjoyed her, and felt yet another shift in their relationship.

'Don't judge me,' she told him. 'You offered.'

She ate the spoonful of mousse, swallowed, then drank from her glass of water. A second later, she stood, regal as ever, and smiled. 'Thank you for asking.'

'I should thank you for accepting,' he replied, taking her hand and leading her to the dance floor.

In movements that should have been too smooth for him to have done it, he brought her into his arms and began to sway.

'I was certain you were going to say no,' he said.

'Why?'

He'd wanted this, hadn't he? A moment to speak with her and find out why she had been acting strangely these last few minutes. But now that he had the opportunity…he didn't want to take it. He didn't want to hear whatever it was because it was sure to upset her, and she wasn't upset now.

Or was she?

Now that he was paying attention, he could

feel the tension in her body. It was slight, but clear. She held herself away from him. Not enough to make it seem weird as they danced, but enough to make it obvious that she wanted distance. But it didn't seem as if she was doing it for *him*. It seemed as if…as if she was doing it for someone else.

'Did someone say something to you?'

The tension in her body became much clearer. Her stiffening very much directed towards him now.

'What do you mean?'

Her voice was too high, too false for him to buy the act.

'Brooke,' he said softly. 'You don't have to pretend. You can tell me.'

The music swelled, their bodies shifted, and he wished he could focus on the conversation instead of her proximity.

Her scent filled his nostrils, more exotic than the one she usually wore, but somehow still entirely her. The heat coming from her body felt as if it had permeated his skin, settling in his body in a way that wasn't normal, but didn't feel foreign. One of her hands was in his, her other rested on his shoulder, and despite the distance between them he was thrilled she was so close.

The last time had been at the beach, and that had been an accident. This was intentional.

She'd consented. It was a heady sensation, that knowledge. It didn't make sense at all, and yet he felt it.

'Someone said we looked...'

She trailed off. Her hand tightened in his. He didn't think she noticed.

'Close. As if we were...married.'

It took him a moment. 'They asked if we were married?'

'Assumed, actually.'

If she hadn't been in his arms, he would have sworn. 'I'm sorry, Brooke. I thought I'd made it clear to people that we aren't together.'

She met his eyes. There was a faint sheen in them. Not tears, but emotion. Powerful emotion that made him feel foolish for not anticipating this. The assumption and her reaction.

'Why are you apologising?' she asked. 'You *have* made it clear. Not once have you said that you and I are together.'

'I should have protected you from—'

'What?' she interrupted. 'The logical assumptions people might make in this kind of situation?'

'Yes,' he said desperately. 'Maybe I shouldn't have brought you here. I wouldn't have if I'd known it would cause you pain.'

'It hasn't caused me pain.'

'What?'

'I'm not upset that someone assumed we were in a relationship.'

She said the words as if they were simple. They were not. Not to him.

'I was more upset that when she realised her mistake, she said we must be close because we're friends. We're not,' she said softly. 'You're my employee.'

'Not really though,' he replied, because he couldn't help it.

'I'm paying you, which I'm certain means we're not friends.'

'That money is going to my sister, Brooke.' Since he already had no self-control, he let go of her hand to brush her chin with his thumb. 'So try again. Think of another reason why you and I can't be...' he hesitated '...friends.'

If she noticed his hesitation she didn't show it. She only stared up at him, her gaze open and disarming.

'The power dynamics—'

'What power dynamics? I. Don't. Work. For. You.'

She exhaled. 'Why are you making this so complicated?'

'I thought I was simplifying it.'

'No.' She shook her head.

He dropped his hand from her face, but only so he could take hers again.

'No, Tyler. Nothing about this is simple.'

'Because of your husband?'

She made a strangled noise, but didn't deny it.

'Okay,' he said. 'We can work with that.'

'We?'

'Relationships generally work that way.'

'You are trying to kill me tonight,' she muttered.

He chuckled. 'Friendships are relationships, too.'

'And, of course, you and I will only ever be friends.'

His heart did a little twirl in his chest. Because if she was saying that, she clearly believed that whatever was happening between them wouldn't stop at friendship.

He didn't understand why he felt happy about it. She was right: this situation *was* complicated. He managed to remind himself of that whenever he needed to. Except now, apparently.

But this was Brooke. The woman who had stayed in his mind for five years after one week together. This was Brooke, the most beautiful woman he'd ever seen. She was kind and generous, and not only to people who knew her. She'd allowed him to continue working in her home because she understood Tia's position. She had been wonderful with all these people tonight, even when they'd asked questions that had made her feel uncomfortable.

'I'm okay with friendship,' he said, meeting her eyes. Because he would be okay with having anything—*anything*—with her. And wasn't that dangerous, too?

She studied him, then sighed and closed the distance between them. She put her head on his chest. 'Of course you are,' she said, so softly she probably thought he hadn't heard her. 'You're much too perfect not to be.'

He wasn't sure if that was a slight or a compliment. From her, he would take either.

He wasn't perfect. Brooke was certain about that. But the words had left her mouth when really, she'd meant to say *of course* he would be okay with friendship. He would try to understand her complicated emotions, not push her, and be content with what she could offer.

It stayed with her long after they said goodbye that night. And it kept her awake. That was okay though. It meant she was up to do an early walk with Mochi, as she'd promised him. As she got ready, she decided he deserved more than a simple walk. She would give him scenery.

Except she hadn't done it before because she wasn't entirely sure she could handle Mochi in unfamiliar terrains. What if he got too excited?

What if he saw another dog and ran off and she lost him?

The thought sent an uncomfortable wave of despair through her. As if sensing it, Mochi whined at her feet.

'Yeah, buddy,' she said, lowering her hand to give him belly rubs. 'I know.'

He barked.

She was pretty sure he hadn't really said anything with that bark, but she frowned. 'No, that wouldn't be appropriate,' she said.

He barked again.

'Mochi, we can't just ask him if he wants to go with us. He probably has plans.'

Mochi didn't make a sound then, only gave her a pitying glance that had her heaving a sigh and reaching for her phone. She assumed the number the agency had given her was Tia's, so she messaged her, asking for Tyler's number.

She got it almost immediately, with no questions or judgement. Which somehow, in itself, felt like a judgement. Because of course she didn't *need* Tyler with her. She could have asked Dom. He would have readily agreed. But then she'd have had to talk about things she didn't want to talk about.

He would almost certainly have mentioned the man working for her—it was in his nature as a police officer—and she would almost certainly have given a suspicious answer, or done something equally mortifying like blush, and he would have known something was up.

And the minute Dom knew, Sierra, his wife, would know. And then her mom would know, and her dad, and it would become a thing when it wasn't a thing. It might never be a thing.

Tyler, with all his complications, was better than facing that.

It took her a long time to figure out what to type. In the end, she just put:

Do you want to come with me and Mochi for a walk? Brooke.

Seconds later, he replied.

June and I will be there in twenty minutes.

She stared at the message, wondered if she'd made a bad decision. If she had, it was clearly becoming a pattern. She had done the same thing the previous night. Spoken before she could really think it through. Which meant she needed to spur herself into action before she could think at all.

She pulled on some comfortable clothing, went downstairs to put on coffee. Mochi hadn't eaten that morning, and she wouldn't feed him until they were done with the walk so there was no chance of an accident in the car. But she gave him water, grabbed a granola bar and was eating it when the doorbell rang.

'You know you have a key, right?' she asked as she opened it.

He smiled. Damn him and his smiles. It was as if he knew how much they affected her. It didn't help that he looked as amazing in casual wear as he had in the suit he'd worn the night before.

No, that wasn't true. He looked great now, but he'd looked amazing last night.

It was entirely possible that she was conflating that observation with the way he'd made her feel. Dancing with him had been an *experience*. And now he was smiling at her as if he wanted her to remember the feel of his hand on her waist. Or the way he'd brushed his thumb over her chin…

'I won't use the key unless it's for work.'

'I appreciate that.' She looked down and found June, staring up at her adoringly. She lowered. 'Hey, girl. How are you?'

The dog immediately pushed her snout into Brooke's hands, before leaning against her for more rubs. Brooke laughed even as she fell over.

'June,' Tyler said in quiet command.

'No, no, it's okay. I understand.' She gave June a cuddle. 'You're just excited to see a new friend, huh? You can probably smell Mochi, too.'

'Where is he?'

'Out back.' She took the hand Tyler offered to help her up. 'Should we get them together?'

'Yeah,' he said, even though he was still staring at her and hadn't let go.

'Tyler?'

'Yeah?'

'You're staring,' she pointed out, even though saying it made her blush.

'Sorry.'

He sounded sheepish. She sucked in her bottom lip to keep herself from smiling. She could do nothing about the warmth fizzing in her stomach though, like the champagne they'd drunk the night before.

'Can I take her out back?' he asked.

'Sure,' she said, letting them both in. 'Do you want some coffee?'

'I'd love some.'

'I can put them in to-go cups. I've accumulated some over the years.'

'Yeah, sure.' He started walking towards the back door, but turned before he could open it. 'Is that something we have to talk about? Why you've accumulated to-go coffee cups over the years?'

'No.' The tone sounded too bright even to her. 'Why would we need to talk about that?'

He chuckled, walked out, and then the barking started and she could no longer hear his voice.

'That,' she said under her breath, 'is a problem.'

The fact that she wanted to hear his voice, that she felt as if she'd lost something because she couldn't... She couldn't feel that way. She knew it, although the reasons for it now seemed hazier.

What had changed that she was suddenly giving it, *him*, space in her head? Had it been that moment at dinner when she'd spoken to his sister? Or afterwards, at the beach, when he'd held her and she'd no longer been able to deny that there was a spark between them? And if things hadn't changed then, they certainly had the night he'd helped her wash Mochi. Or even last night, when he'd asked her to be his friend.

The truth was that all of those things had contributed to the change, and she knew it. A better question was *how* had things changed? Yes, she'd offered to accompany him to his business function and called him to join her when she took her dog for a walk. But she still felt... Not uneasy, but not entirely comfortable either.

Some of that might be because she was trying to figure out something completely new. Friendship or something more, it didn't matter. She hadn't forged either since Kian's death. And that 'something more' part made things messier.

She had been moving her life forward. She *had*. But this was different from moving house or getting a new job. This was...personal.

'Well, they're fast friends.'

She whirled around, spilling the hot coffee she'd been pouring into a cup over her wrist. She dealt with the situation swiftly, setting down both the coffee and the cup and going to the sink.

Tyler met her there, all concern and care. 'I shouldn't have scared you like that,' he said, taking her hand and putting it under cool running water.

'It's fine.'

But it wasn't. Because she was quite sure the burning she felt in her wrist wasn't because of the coffee.

'Do you scare easily?' he asked.

'Not usually.'

'So just when I'm here?' He offered her a wry smile.

'No. *No*,' she emphasised with a shake of her head. 'I was thinking about something. I got distracted, that's all. It has very little to do with you.'

He made a sound that made her think he knew it had a lot to do with him, but he didn't correct her. Instead he turned off the water and disappeared to find the first-aid box. As she waited, she inspected her wrist. It was rcd, a little sensitive, but nothing some aloe gel couldn't fix.

The lingering tingles from him touching her, however, were harder to shake off. Especially when he returned and gently smoothed the gel over the offending area.

She couldn't help but watch him as he did it. He was frowning, his eyes focused on her wrist, his lips lightly pursed. Even with an expression of concentration he was good-looking. His features were so rough that his concern almost seemed out of place. Except it wasn't. He wore his concern for those he cared about as if it were a second skin. In fact, nothing about his personality coincided with his looks.

A big, muscular, dangerous-looking man like him might easily have had a big, muscular, dangerous personality. But he was charming. Kind. Generous. He was thoughtful and good with dogs and everything about him made her...

She blinked when her eyes began to fill up. She must have made a sound because he glanced up and immediately removed his hands.

'Did I hurt you?'

'No.' But then she realised he was giving her an out and she should take it. 'I mean, yes. Not you, just it. It's painful.'

And it was—but not her wrist. This. Moving forward. It was painful, and that was why it was so messy.

'Brooke,' he said, moving his hands completely away from her wrist now and cupping her face. 'What's wrong?'

'Nothing.'

'Tell that to your eyes.'

He brushed away a tear she hadn't realised was falling. She bit her bottom lip. This wasn't supposed to be happening. None of this was supposed to be happening. She just wanted to take her dog for a walk, for heaven's sake. She didn't need to be punished for that.

Punished?

She didn't know where that word had come from, and she didn't have a chance to think about it when he was so close. He smelled like an early-morning breeze and man, a wholly Tyler smell that was part of what made all this so difficult.

'It's a walk with a friend, Brooke. Nothing more.'

'I know. I know.'

'Good. Okay.'

But then he leaned his forehead against hers, something so intimate that she closed her eyes, trying to gain some measure of control over her emotions.

'It isn't any more than that, okay.'

She opened her eyes. 'You already said that.'

'I know.' He pulled away with a small smile. 'I thought we could both do with the reminder.'

CHAPTER NINE

THE SUN WAS barely in the sky when they got to the park Brooke had suggested, but the air was already starting to warm.

'I don't think we'll be able to stay for long,' Brooke murmured, getting out of the car before helping Mochi out.

'No,' Tyler agreed. 'We should have about an hour under the trees.' He tightened his grip on June's leash. 'This was a good choice.'

'Thank you.' She smiled brightly. 'I did some research.'

'You haven't actually brought Mochi here before?'

'No.' She gave the dog an absent pat on the head. 'We haven't done many outings beyond our usual walk. I…' She trailed off, adjusting her cap. 'This is going to sound like a confession, and I guess it kind of is, but I swear I didn't only invite you because of that. I could have asked my brother—' She broke off.

One of his favourite things about Brooke was

when she got carried away. She realised it too late, and by then, he had all the information he could possibly want about a situation.

'I'm afraid Mochi will see something or some-one that interests him and he'll run off and I won't be able to control him.'

It took a second, then he caught up. 'So you asked me along because you thought I'd be able to control him better?'

She quirked a brow. 'You have a way with him. It must be all that *authority*.'

He chuckled and they began to walk. It was a gorgeous day despite the heat, and the place she had chosen really was beautiful. A large sign designated the trail, with trees rising high and curling over the path. A silver railing kept the explosion of nature on the right at bay, and the green of it made everything seem cool as it surrounded a stream that ran alongside the trail. The water wasn't deep—if he had to guess, he thought it would probably reach his knee—and it was clear, affording them a good view of the pebbles, large and small, that sat beneath the surface.

Further down would be a river, he knew, but he didn't think they'd get there. Not if they wanted to keep the dogs and themselves from overheating.

'Mochi needs to fit into your life, not the other way around,' he told her.

'I know that,' she said. 'But my life before would never have entailed walking park trails, so it's all about balance.'

'It wouldn't?' He set an easy pace, which seemed to work for all four of them. 'What would it have entailed?'

'Before Mochi?' she asked.

He nodded.

She thought about it for a long time, stopping for Mochi to smell a branch that had fallen from one of the trees. 'Mostly work, I guess. Occasionally, on a Saturday, I'd go to one of the food markets and get some things to eat for the weekend.'

'Mochi could do that with you.'

'Yeah, but what happens if he sees a little kid and gets excited?' she asked. 'I'd be banned for life.'

'So we need to work on you controlling him.' He stopped. As he did so, June sat down, looking up at him for guidance. 'Like this.'

Brooke looked down at June, then back at him. 'How could you have possibly taught her that already? You haven't even had her for that long. And she's a stray.'

'Dogs learn pretty quickly, especially if you're consistent. This is pretty basic, really. Get him to walk with you, to stop with you. That foundation will help you to control him more when he's around other dogs and people.' He eyed Mochi, who was, to his credit, walking well. 'This is already pretty different to the way he was walking when we bumped into you a couple of weeks ago.'

'I think the two walks a day are helping with his energy,' she admitted sheepishly. 'I feel silly for not realising he needed it before.'

'Don't feel silly,' Tyler said. 'Just figure out what he needs. Do some research on his breed.'

'He's mixed.'

'Well, he looks part collie to me, and that breed is notoriously energetic. Two walks are the bare minimum.' At her stricken look, he laughed. 'You play with him in the garden, don't you?'

'Yes.'

'Well, that's another way for him to get out his energy. And the good news is he's a smart dog. He'll learn pretty quickly. Here—let's swap and I'll show you.'

He took Mochi from her and started with basic sit and stand commands. He'd brought treats for June, and Mochi was greedy, so it didn't take him long to learn. And then they walked.

As he did all this, Tyler talked it through with Brooke. After a little while, he had her take Mochi. That required slightly more work.

'You're asking him to sit, not telling him.'

'If someone just *told* me to sit, I wouldn't feel

very good about that,' she argued. 'But if they *asked* me, I would welcome it.'

'Brooke,' he said, mustering all his patience while simultaneously fighting a smile, 'he's a dog. He doesn't want to be asked. He wants to be told and to be rewarded for doing what he's told. You're his Alpha.'

She narrowed her eyes. 'Again with this Alpha business?'

He didn't fight the smile. 'It's nature.'

'Sure,' she replied darkly. 'Most things in the male understanding of the world seem to be based on "nature."'

'I'm pretty sure the right answer here is for me to apologise for all of mankind.'

'Apology accepted,' she said primly, but she offered him a small smile.

She put more authority into her tone after that. When it worked, she gave him a dark look, as if to say *Don't you dare say I told you so*. He lifted his hand in surrender. He didn't have to say it. The fact that he was grinning like a stupid person told her as much.

He preferred this to what had happened that morning. When her vulnerability had been so raw it hurt his heart as if it were nails on a chalkboard. Things seemed to switch effortlessly between easy and hard with them. If he were inclined to, he might say that was part of what made it special between them. But he wasn't inclined to. Because her reaction that morning had reminded him of the stakes.

Oh, he'd been intent on charming her. The night before, when she'd been in his arms, once again displaying that vulnerability, he'd promised her they would be friends. He'd believed it would be a foundation between them for something else. Something bigger. But there were too many factors at play.

He'd left that function the night before even more confused about what he wanted to do. Well, no. He knew what he *wanted* to do. He was just conflicted about it. He couldn't leave Tia and Nyle. No matter how much Brooke assured him it wouldn't be abandonment, he didn't believe it. Perhaps because it wasn't her assurance he needed—it was Tia's. And getting it would involve telling Tia about the business opportunity, which he wasn't ready to do.

While he was dealing with all that he *couldn't* lay a foundation for anything more than friendship with Brooke. Not only because he couldn't offer her the certainty she deserved, but because if he left he would be leaving her, too. How could he do that to her? He wasn't his father; he wouldn't leave the people he cared about.

He'd told her once that employees and employers could be friends, and he believed that. Now he wished he didn't. Now he wished he'd left his desire for her locked behind the pretence of professionalism. Now he wished he didn't have any past with her complicating things.

They reached a break in the path and made their way to a bench in a small, open grassy area. He was thankful for the reprieve from walking. Maybe because he was hoping it would give him one from his thoughts, too.

'This is probably a good place to turn around,' Brooke said as she lowered to give the dogs water. 'After a break.'

'You need a break?' He forced himself to tease her. 'I could do this for ever.'

She stuck out her tongue, before taking off her cap and drinking some water herself. A bead escaped the bottle, trailing over her chin, down her neck, before disappearing into her cleavage. He'd done his utmost not to notice that cleavage when he'd got to her house that morning. In truth, it was perfectly respectable. Except he couldn't look at her and respond in a perfectly respectable way.

He remembered too clearly the gentle swell of her breasts in that gold dress, the material hugging her curves, the colour seemingly designed for her skin.

He couldn't only blame it on that though. Everything about her made his body react. She could be wearing a black bin bag and face paint and he'd still be dying to hold her in his arms, caress her. So the tight top meant to support her breasts as she walked would inevitably distract him.

He wanted to follow the trail of that water with his tongue. He didn't care that her skin had a light sheen of sweat. She would taste of salt and Brooke and he couldn't think of anything he wanted more.

He exhaled sharply, pulled his own water from his backpack and drank like a dying man. He felt as if he *were* dying. How else could he describe his response when he had only just thought about all the reasons he needed to have boundaries with her? When he'd been doing so from the beginning of their reunion?

'Uh-oh,' Brooke said softly.

His head turned. She was looking at his face, so it was unlikely she was noticing his body's reaction. Good. He wouldn't be able to explain that after he'd assured her they were only friends.

'What?' he said, once he'd got his thinking under control.

'You're having a Brooke moment.'

'What does that mean?'

'Well, it's good that you ask because it could mean a number of things. The one I'm currently thinking about has nothing to do with the patriarchy—' she gave him a small smile '—but with getting lost in your own head.'

'I'm not—' He broke off with a sigh. 'I am. I thought about something and it unravelled quickly.'

'That's how it happens, I'm afraid.' She patted his hand. 'One moment you're thinking about how cute a guy is, the next you're remembering your deceased husband and wondering if he'd be okay with you thinking about how cute another guy is.'

'Is that what happened this morning?'

'Oh, no,' she said, shaking her head with a laugh. 'I'm not falling for that.'

He stared, but she didn't elaborate. For a minute he deliberated about whether he should push, but her expression told him it wasn't a good idea.

'You're really not going answer that?' he asked.

'Nope.'

'At least confirm that I'm the cute guy?'

'You're not,' she said. 'I was talking about the guy who helped take my groceries to the car the other day. He even called me "ma'am," which made me feel old, but also made me feel kind of fancy.'

She twisted her shoulder in an endearing way and he smiled. How could he not be delighted by her? She drew him in—no, locked him in, really—and he was so enamoured that he'd handed her the key.

'You should stop doing this,' he said. He meant to tease, but his tone was serious.

'What?'

'Being so…so *you*.'

She studied him. 'I would be offended if it weren't for that look on your face. It's telling me that you're actually complimenting me.'

'Yeah.' His hand lifted to twirl the ends of her hair around his finger. He stopped when he realised what he was doing. 'Sorry. I—'

He didn't finish, and she reached up and caught his hand. 'You know what I think would solve a lot of this tension? If we kissed.'

'You… Excuse me?'

'Get it out of the way. Out of our systems, you know?' She barrelled on. 'If we both want it, of course. If not, I'll gladly never speak of—'

He was kissing her before she could finish.

CHAPTER TEN

GETTING DESIRE OUT of their systems might have been one of the reasons they were kissing, but Brooke knew there was more to it. For both of them. Though she was sure their reasons were different.

For her, it was the tension. It danced between them. Sometimes to a slow and lingering beat, almost harmless in its laziness; other times the beat was sharp and passionate, demanding to be heeded. Today, both those beats had played in her.

And then there was this.

An utterly irresistible rhythm that neither of them could ignore.

It didn't seem to matter that she'd thought of a long list of reasons as to why kissing him was a bad idea. All of them were very much still valid, but she thought some of her problem lay in curiosity. What would it be like to kiss him? To kiss any man, really?

Though even as she thought it she knew that was a lie. It wasn't her curiosity to kiss *any* man that was causing her internal conflict. It was her curiosity to kiss *Tyler*. To find out if she was ready to move on with him.

So now they were kissing.

A nice, simple way of sorting through her feelings.

How she was only figuring out that was a lie now, as she was kissing him, was anyone's guess.

It was an overload of sensations. The gentle press of his lips against hers…the way he dropped her hand to cup her face… Their lips moved tentatively against one another. Testing, tasting, teasing. If somehow they'd been transported to the stream beside them, submerged in water, she wouldn't have been surprised. Every single movement felt as slow and deliberate as if they were under water. Every breath she took felt hard-won, her lungs no longer working as they normally did.

But they seemed to be adjusting to this new reality. To being under water. Hell, she might be turning into a mermaid. If so, he would definitely be the prince she sacrificed her voice for. It was a choice she would gladly make if it meant she could keep kissing him.

Of course, when she was rational again, she would protest against the idea of sacrificing anything for the sake of a kiss. But he had just swept his tongue into her mouth and heat was curling in her belly and she was ready to do whatever she needed to do to keep these sensations coming.

Even if it meant losing her sanity.

A part of her was aware of what was happening. It was because of that overload of sensation. With the lick of his tongue, it was as if something inside her began to inflate, more and more, until she was certain she was floating up into the sky. It wasn't a bad thing. At least, it didn't feel that way right now. It felt like a gift. The way his hand moved down from her face to her neck, over her collarbone, down her arm… The way it moved to her hip, lingered on her waist, settled on her ribs.

Higher, she thought. But the bottom of her breast was already touching his hand and she thought she might lose her mind. She could only imagine what would happen if he actually touched her skin, stroked her like she wanted him to.

The heat in her belly would boil, overflow, trail a pathway down to her core. For the moment that ache between her legs was a pulsing need. It was as if her body had separated her desire into the heat in her stomach and the pulsing between her thighs. Probably to save her. Because the moment those things converged, she would lose herself completely. And if she did that she would do something insane. Like straddle him, placing his desire against hers and checking whether, together, they could sate their appetite for one another.

The thought was as good as a bucket of ice over her. She pulled back, leaning away until she was at the edge of the bench. Tyler did the same at his end. Both of them stared. With a trembling hand, she traced her lips. Why did they suddenly feel like the scene of a crime? As if they'd done something illegal and were waiting to be caught?

Mochi tugged at his leash, reminding Brooke that he was still there. She looked down, amazed that she had managed to keep hold of him when her world had completely and utterly changed.

'Yeah,' she said softy. 'Yeah, let's go.'

She stood, her legs feeling weak and unstable beneath her.

'Brooke,' Tyler said.

When she turned, she found him standing behind her.

'Are you okay?'

'Sure.' She offered him a smile that she was sure wasn't very convincing. 'Are you?'

'Yes. Except I feel like you're lying to me.'

He lifted a hand and curled it around her ear, as if she had hair there. But she'd tied her hair up that morning, and she knew what he was doing was more to touch her than anything else.

She resisted the urge to close her eyes, to sigh. Instead, she moved back. Gently. It didn't matter how she'd done it though, she realised as a flash of hurt crossed his face. His reaction would have been the same regardless.

'I'm not lying.'

'Brooke—'

'Tyler,' she replied deliberately. The look of expectation on his face didn't change. She sighed. 'Give me time, okay? I need...a moment.'

'So you're not okay?'

'Are *you*?' she challenged. 'Because you pressing me now feels like an excuse to not face your own feelings about what happened.'

Junc whined, and Tyler gave her an absent-minded rub on the head. 'Maybe we both need time.'

'Yes,' she agreed.

Not waiting for him to say anything further, she began to walk.

By the time they reached the car they were both sweaty messes. At some point during their walk, the sun had got much hotter. They'd had to stop to give the dogs water often, and it had taken longer to get back than it had to get to the grassy area.

'You can drive,' Brooke said, throwing him the keys. 'I'm not sure I'm capable of that yet.'

His smile was crooked and a little reserved. She understood. Hell, she deserved it. She had pushed him away, quite deliberately, and now she was pretending it hadn't happened.

But some time during the walk back her fear had melted into something else. Guilt, mostly. She could have reacted better about the kiss. She should have. Except her legs had been shaking, along with some other choice parts of her body, and she hadn't been able to deal with that *and* force herself to have a logical conversation.

But that wasn't his fault. Well, her emotional reaction wasn't his fault. The physical reaction… Her entire body clenched at the memory, as if somehow tightening her muscles would prevent the sensations from gripping her.

Without thought, she looked at Tyler. Part of her wanted to check whether he was experiencing these aftershocks, too. Apparently not. He seemed perfectly calm, his face holding a serene expression despite the turmoil of what had happened before their walk back. Despite the slight sheen on his face and his body from the exertion of their walk.

She tried not to pay attention to the sweat that was still periodically rolling down her back and in between her breasts.

'What's wrong?' he asked.

She frowned. 'Nothing. Why?'

'You're looking at me and fanning yourself.'

She looked down. Saw that she had, indeed, been lifting her top as if she were fanning herself.

It was all perfectly innocent, and yet it looked incredibly incriminating.

'I was thinking that you look all cool and calm while I'm sweating buckets. The fanning was a thoughtless response.'

'Hmm.'

She rolled her eyes at the disbelieving sound, but couldn't help the tickle of a smile at her mouth. Because she could understand what he was thinking. If the roles had been reversed, she would have thought the exact same thing.

'I work out a lot,' was his next comment.

'I figured.' The flick of his gaze made her realise what she was saying. She didn't bother hiding her reaction. 'You look like you do.'

'How do I look?'

'Not falling for that.'

He gave a soft chuckle. 'Looks aren't exactly a good criteria for working out, but if we're going to use them, I'd say you work out a lot, too.'

She refused to blush. 'You're trying to make me say something weird again, which is entirely possible, yes, but I'm not going to fall for it.'

'It was a compliment.'

'You know as well as I do that I do not "work out a lot."'

'How would I know that?'

'One, I work too much for "a lot." Two, that gold dress didn't hide much.'

'It didn't, did it?' He gave her a sly look. 'It's almost as if someone bought it with that very thing in mind.'

She laughed because he was teasing, and because she preferred this to the silence of their walk. It was unfair of her. How could she want him to be like this when she didn't like where it led? Teasing led to flirting—hell, they might already be flirting now—and flirting led to touches, to kisses.

With the way that man kissed, it would lead to other things that she was in no way prepared for.

But then, she would have thought she wasn't prepared for Tyler *at all* a few weeks ago. She'd been ready to get out there, to move on then, but thinking about it and doing it were entirely different.

Her plan had involved arranging drinks with friends she hadn't seen in while. Or going to a bar by herself. Anything that would have moved her personal life forward *slowly*.

The plan certainly wouldn't have looked like this. This fast and almost inevitable progression of whatever was happening between her and Tyler, as if they'd forged some kind of a foundation long before.

Even with Kian, when she had been young and nothing in her life had cautioned her against falling, the pace had been slower. They'd been friends first, then they'd started dating. Weeks later had come the first kiss. It had been months later before anything more happened.

If she could ask whoever was in charge of controlling these things some questions, she would ask what that meant. Did the fact that she had fallen for her husband in slow and subtle ways mean what she was feeling for Tyler now was dangerous? Her relationship with Kian had been the most significant thing in her life—surely anything that didn't feel like that meant it wasn't worth pursuing?

But what about that feeling of inevitability? Because with Kian she had felt very much in control. With Tyler…she did not. That felt significant, too.

It was what scared the hell out of her.

'Brooke?'

She looked at him.

'We're here.'

They were indeed in front of her house.

'Right.'

This was her chance to escape. To put some distance between them so she could think about what had happened last night, this morning. She could give herself a chance to catch up with 'the inevitability'—if that was what she was going to call it.

So heaven only knew why she said, 'Do you want to come inside for breakfast?'

The invitation came as a surprise. More surprising was the fact that she offered him a shower, clean clothing—he tried not to think about the fact that it might have been her husband's—and the spare bedroom on the ground floor to change.

He appreciated all of it. He wanted a chance to speak to her about what had happened. If breakfast didn't give him that chance, at the very least it would help him reassure her that she had nothing to worry about.

Which was a lie since he was worried himself. He was trying not to think about the reasons for that.

Priorities. Your family. Your job. And those two seem interchangeable since you're considering leaving your only family for a job.

He wasn't succeeding very well, clearly. But it did serve as a reminder that he had enough problems; he didn't need to add Brooke to the list.

Yet here he was, getting ready to take a shower in the en suite bathroom in her spare bedroom.

He put the water on, let it heat while he went to grab clothes from the bedroom. And paused when he saw Brooke there.

They stared at one another for a moment. Him because he hadn't expected her to be there, let alone with a handful of toiletries. Her, probably because he'd already stripped down to his underwear.

'I am so sorry,' she said, whirling around.

In the process, one of the bottles in her hand went flying against the opposite wall.

'I heard the shower, and I thought you were already in it. I was just going to leave these things here because I didn't want you not to have deodorant or lotion. I did not expect to find you almost naked. I am so sorry. I am so, *so* sorry.'

He was grinning by the end of it, though he probably should be feeling a little more compassion for her situation.

'It's okay,' he said easily, refusing the temptation to tease her. 'I appreciate you bringing me all that stuff. It's almost like being in a hotel.'

'Except in a hotel, you get privacy.' She nearly turned back, but stopped herself before she could. 'If you go in the shower, I'll leave these things on the bed, okay?'

'Okay.'

He was still smiling when he went into the shower, aware of the fact that she had completely swept all thoughts of priorities out of his mind. It should have been bad. It *was* bad. But she forced him to live in the present. Not in the general *now*, but in the very moment that was happening.

When was the last time he'd ever had that?

When he was younger, probably—except he couldn't pinpoint any moment when that had been true.

Even before his father had left, he'd been concerned about the tremors of unhappiness he'd felt between his parents. He hadn't understood what it truly meant, but he'd known his mother didn't smile as much with his father as she did when she was with Tyler and Tia.

After his father had left he'd been worried about his mother, his sister. Their future had been financially ominous, along with their precarious emotional state after being abandoned by the man who should have taken care of them.

As an adult, he was focused on making himself successful. If he did that, he could take care of his mother and sister's financial fears. Although they would barely let him, which was another concern. It felt as if the past was haunting them. They were both too accustomed to working hard, to not relying on anyone but themselves. They were afraid that relying on anyone, even him, would make them vulnerable again.

So, no, he hadn't lived in the present for a very long time. No wonder Brooke appealed to him so much.

He made quick work of the shower, then used all the toiletries with a grin he knew was stupid before he got dressed.

Brooke was in the kitchen, freshly showered herself, preparing eggs in a bowl.

'Hey,' he said.

'Hey,' she replied, giving him a small smile. Her hands stilled. 'Once again, I want to apologise for—'

'There's nothing to apologise for,' he interrupted firmly. 'It wasn't like you were intentionally hoping to catch me in my underwear.'

'No,' she said, very quickly. 'Not at all.'

If she hadn't been so tense, he would have asked her why. But he could read the room.

'I didn't think so.' He changed the subject before she could get caught up on the details. 'How can I help?'

There was a pause, but then she gave him instructions to help her with the French toast, bacon, scrambled eggs and fruit she was preparing.

'Are you sure that's enough?' he teased, getting the bread.

'Isn't it? I would usually only eat one of the above, but I figured you'd be pretty hungry.'

'Should I be offended by that?'

'You work out a lot,' she said with a wink. 'You probably need the sustenance.'

They worked in tandem, easily helping one another out. Tyler noticed that she was avoiding touching him. Hell, she was actively trying not to be in his space at all. She seemed to be doing it without thinking, shifting when he shifted, moving when he moved, as if she had some radar when he was in her space and adjusted accordingly.

It took him a moment, but he realised he had an internal radar when it came to her, too. Attraction. When she came close to him, the heat from her body sank into him until every part of him was saturated. If it wasn't the heat, it was the awareness, skidding over his skin, causing every hair on his body to stand on end.

If she felt that, too, then she was simply avoiding those physical feelings. And he couldn't be upset about that. One, because she was clearly responding out of instinct. Two, because she felt it. Something. Anything... Of course he knew that she did. She'd instigated that kiss; she'd responded during that kiss.

He took a deep sip from his water, remembering that response. The little moan she'd given when their tongues had touched; her shudder when he'd skimmed her skin; her exhalation when his fingers had sunk into the flesh at her hips...

Another gulp of water reminded him that now wasn't the time to think about it. Now he wanted to make her feel better that it had happened—and that certainly wouldn't be the case if he started responding physically to the memory of it.

'I'm sure I've told you this before, but you're really good in the kitchen,' she said.

'My mom forced both me and Tia to be,' he replied, grateful for the reprieve from his thoughts. 'The household chores were a team effort. We'd rotate cooking and cleaning between the three of us after my father left.'

She was waiting to flip the last of the French toast, so she had the opportunity to study him. He felt her gaze pierce through him, even though he was standing so she couldn't see his face.

'You guys really were a unit,' she said.

'Yeah.'

'It must have been hard when your mom died.'

'It was.' He paused, letting the wave of grief roll over him. He didn't try to hide it. Out of all the people in the world, he was certain she would understand. 'She had a heart attack in her sleep. I found her one morning.'

'*You* found her?'

'Rather me than Tia,' he said, hearing the compassion in her voice. 'I could handle it better than she could.'

'Yeah?' she asked. 'Is that something she's said to you, or is that your perception of the situation?'

He frowned. 'Does it matter?'

'I guess not,' she said thoughtfully. 'But my gut tells me that it's the latter, and that it's the same reason you haven't told her about your business opportunity. You think she can't handle it. And where has that thinking brought you, exactly?'

CHAPTER ELEVEN

'OH!' BROOKE EXCLAIMED as soon as she said the words. 'That was much more personal than I intended on getting.'

'You think?'

At the dry note in Tyler's voice, she winced. She placed the final slice of French toast on a plate and turned to face him. His expression didn't look upset, more pensive.

She slid the plate over to him. 'Truce?'

His gaze flickered down. 'You're offering me an entire plate of French toast to make up for saying something that might be true?'

'Only if it works,' she replied. She waited a beat. 'Might be true, huh?'

She couldn't describe the look he gave her as a glare, but it wasn't entirely a positive one.

She pushed the plate closer to him.

He narrowed his eyes, but she could see the faintest twitch at his lips.

'You can't bribe me with food.'

'I'm not bribing you,' she said truthfully. 'I'm comforting you.'

'I don't need to be comforted.'

'Well, in that case...'

She reached out to take the plate back, but he snatched it up into the air. It was so unexpected that she gave a startled laugh, before lifting her hands in surrender.

'Fair is fair.'

Seconds later he set the plate down next to the eggs and bacon he'd already fried. She'd meant it when she'd told him he was good in the kitchen. Much more efficient than she was. But she had managed to put the coffee on before he'd come out of the shower, and...

Her brain paused for a moment as she remembered walking into the spare room when she'd thought he was in the shower. She'd only seen him for a few seconds, but it had been enough to make an impact. She knew he worked out, knew he was built, but the man had muscles in places she wasn't sure should have muscles.

She had never found that kind of build attractive before—she preferred tall and lean—but apparently she'd been waiting for Tyler.

And really, that should make her ashamed of her superficiality. Oddly enough, she didn't feel bad at all.

'Coffee?' she asked, hoping he wouldn't somehow pick up on the lust in her voice.

'It's too hot for that.'

She turned. 'Too hot for coffee? A life-giving liquid?'

He smirked. For some reason it made her think about how he looked in his underwear again. She shoved the thought out of her mind.

'I know it's unbelievable. Do you have something colder? Juice?'

'Of course.'

She got the juice out, poured him some, then suggested they eat outside. After they'd put all the food on the table and settled in under the veranda, silence stretched over them. It was the kind of silence that came after a hard day of work: quiet, content, comfortable. Almost as peaceful as their dogs laying beneath one of the trees in the garden, exhausted from their morning activities.

She hadn't thought that, after what had happened between them that morning, they'd be able to share something like this. It made her think of the inevitability between them, and tension rolled in her stomach.

It was so unknown, all of this, and she couldn't comprehend it. There were times when she felt that she must. That she would suffer if she couldn't figure it all out. But at other times, when she didn't think about it, only allowed herself to *be*, it didn't matter at all.

She released a breath, striving for the latter. If only to make it through their breakfast together.

'When my dad left I did assume a lot of responsibility at home.'

She turned, not nearly as surprised that he'd broken the silence as she might have been if she weren't so aware of him. He'd obviously been thinking about what she'd said in the kitchen. His contemplative expression, his silence, the stiff way he held his body, told her as much.

So she didn't interrupt, only let him work it out.

'Now I'm wondering if that happened because my mom and Tia needed me, or because I decided they needed me.'

She tilted her head. 'Could it be both?'

He blinked. 'Yeah, I guess.'

She gave him a moment. Or maybe she was giving herself a moment to decide whether she wanted to say what she was thinking.

'Just say it,' he said, a smile playing at his lips as he studied her.

'Only if I get immunity?'

He lifted his eyes to the sky, but nodded.

'I don't think it's a bad thing, caring for your family. Especially during something as traumatic as abandonment. But... How can you think what you want to do is the same as what your father did?'

'He took a job in a different country.'

'And that is literally the only thing this situation and his have in common.' She paused. 'Unless you plan on not coming back? On leaving Tia and her son to fend for themselves?' She waited for it to settle. 'I don't know the details of what happened,' she added gently, 'but it sounds like that's what your father did, and that's what you want to avoid.'

There was a long, drawn-out silence. Eventually, Tyler said, 'He said he was leaving to make our lives better. But they weren't better when he left. Mom was more stressed. He sent money, but she didn't want to use it. It took me a long time to realise it was because she didn't want to give him a reason to stay away.' He scratched the arm of his chair. 'They weren't happy when he was here, but I think… I think she wanted to work on it. And his response was to leave. Things got bad financially, and she had to start using the money, and that…' He shifted his hands, his grip tightening on his chair. 'It made her unhappy. I think she felt like she was conceding something by taking it. Her pride and her marriage.'

'So you're saying that you're not worried about Tia financially,' she said slowly, trying to put all the parts together, 'but emotionally? That if she needs you, you won't be there, and that'll make her unhappy?'

'No...' he said, but he looked doubtful. He sighed. 'I'm worried about her financially *and* emotionally. I don't want her to get to the place my mom was in before she accepted help. While I'm here, at least I can monitor the situation.'

'Or control it?'

'Help her,' he corrected with a wry twist of his mouth. 'Like step in for a job when she needs me to.'

'Have you had to do that before, or is it just this once?'

He didn't answer. But then, he didn't have to; she already knew what he'd say.

'Basically, you're putting your life on pause because of a potential situation that might or might not arise if you leave?'

'It's not that easy.'

'No, it's not,' she agreed. 'And it sounds like the only way you'll figure it out is if you talk with her. She might feel the same way about you, Tyler.' At his confused look, she elaborated. 'She wants *you* to be happy and secure in the same way you want *her* to be happy and secure, I'm sure. Give her a chance to let that happen.'

When he didn't look convinced, she leaned over and rested a hand on his. 'There's nothing wrong with wanting a life where you're important, too.'

His eyes were soft, emotion shimmering through them like a rainbow after a day of rain. Slowly, he tipped over their hands so that his lay on top of hers. It should have been a warning for what he said next. She was fairly certain it was—she had simply ignored it. So when he said his next words she wasn't prepared.

'Is that something I could say to you, too?'

Her response was to open her mouth, stare at him, and eventually say, 'No.'

Tyler didn't reply immediately. Hell, he probably shouldn't have said anything in the first place. But she'd spoken so firmly, so kindly about his situation, completely unaware of how her words applied to her own situation.

He tilted his head. 'You don't think you've been living for someone else these last few years?'

She pulled a face. 'It's not the same thing.'

'Why not?'

'He's not here,' she said, spreading her hands out in front of her. 'How can I be living for him when he's not even here?'

It was such a raw question that he didn't speak. He didn't want to push her, certainly not when, again, some of his intentions were selfish. He wanted her to know that it was okay for her to move on. It didn't have to be with him—*liar*, an inner voice taunted—but moving forward with her life wouldn't be tainting her husband's memory in any way.

Spending that week with me before or after his death though...

He frowned. He'd been successfully ignoring the fact that they had a history together just as she was. Oh, it slipped into his mind here and there, but for the most part he kept to his earlier resolve. This was yet another reason why. If he started thinking about it, he would have an endless number of questions as to why she wasn't addressing it.

Did she not remember it? That seemed impossible, considering what was happening between them now. So why was she still pretending it hadn't happened? The only reason that made sense was if she had been married at that time. And if not married, a freshly grieving widow. If that was the case, she must have been using him. If *either* option was the case, she had been using him.

Their kiss back then must have popped the bubble they were in, bringing her back to the real world. Making her realise what she was doing.

But that didn't seem like the Brooke he knew now. The woman who wouldn't fully utilise the person she had hired to help her in her home, for heaven's sake. Why would she use a stranger to help her forget about her husband?

Except she was reticent about her husband.

He could put it down to grief, but that was an easy solution. A simple one that didn't feel right...

Why did he suddenly feel like ignoring their past was no longer an option?

'I don't like this,' she said. 'I don't like it that you can see things I can't when you barely know anything about the situation.'

'So tell me,' he said quietly. Selfishly. Because now he wanted to know what things had been like with her husband so he could figure out where he'd fitted into the situation.

But she didn't reply, not for a long time, and he thought she might not answer. And if that were the case, he couldn't stay. He'd need to keep to his boundaries then, or at least get some space where he could figure out why he was feeling so out of sorts.

That feeling might easily have come from what he'd revealed—to her and to himself. Mostly to her. Because now, she knew more about him than he could ever hope to know about her. Unless she decided to share. Which, considering she still hadn't responded, was unlikely.

Then she spoke.

'It was a car accident.'

When she looked at him, her eyes reminded him of the ocean during a storm.

'We were driving home from the birthday party of one of Kian's friends and someone ran a red light...' She trailed off, her fingers curling into her skirt. 'His condition was critical since we were hit on his side. Mine wasn't. I barely had any injuries.'

'You were...you were in the car?'

She nodded. 'He spent about a week in the hospital after that, and his heart kept failing. It put his body under so much strain, so I signed a DNR. He...' She cleared her throat. 'He died a couple of hours later.'

'Brooke, I'm...' Speechless. He was speechless. 'I'm sorry.'

'Thanks.'

When she sat back, he realised for the first time that she had moved forward, to the edge of her seat, at some point during the conversation. He wanted to lean over and take her hand, as she had done for him earlier, but since she had been the one to pull away it felt like crossing a line she had drawn.

'The trauma took a long time to work through,' she said, as if there hadn't been a pause after she'd last spoken. 'I had a concussion, which wasn't bad compared to Kian. I lost some of my memories, but he lost…' She met his eyes. 'He lost his life.'

Again, he was reminded of the ocean during a storm. Of the thrashing of waves against rocks, a violence that was evident but seemingly caused no damage and left no scars. What had happened to Brooke had affected her deeply, even though she seemed fine now. But just because no one witnessed how the waves eroded those rocks over time didn't mean the damage wasn't there.

The metaphor tangled his brain into a web for a long time. So long he didn't realise what she'd said until she was already standing, putting the plates together.

'Wait—did you say you lost some of your memories?'

She didn't look at him. 'Yeah.'

'As in…amnesia?'

'Selective,' she confirmed. 'Parts of the accident and some of the time after. A lot of what I've told you my brother told me.'

'You don't remember it? Any of it?'

'I remember bits and pieces. But most of the events surrounding the accident and the week or so after I don't remember. The doctors said it was a result of the physical and emotional trauma of the accident and then losing Kian.' She pulled the plates against her body. 'So, Tyler, if I'm not living for myself, it's because I had a husband who didn't get to live at all. Living for him doesn't feel like a choice now, does it?'

She didn't wait for a reply, moving into the house. He didn't follow her. His mind was too busy spinning. He was afraid that if he did follow her, he would push past the line she'd set. He might be selfish, but he wasn't a complete jerk. Besides, he had a good idea of where all the questions he had would lead.

He'd met Brooke outside the hospital. It must have either been during the week her husband had been in hospital, or after he'd died. And if that was the case, she *didn't* remember any of the time they'd spent together. Not because it didn't mean anything to her, but because she had amnesia.

She didn't remember him because she couldn't.

He would have to tell her…wouldn't he?

Why did that seem like the nuclear option all of a sudden?

CHAPTER TWELVE

BROOKE HADN'T SEEN Tyler in over a week. Not since they'd had that fairly explosive conversation during breakfast. That might not be the right description considering they hadn't exactly had an argument, but it had felt emotionally explosive. And the carnage hadn't only been memories she'd managed to keep at bay for a long time, but apparently their fledgling friendship.

If only she'd known that all she had to do to stop their relationship from progressing faster than she liked was to tell him about her dead husband.

'What?' Dom said now, looking up from a plate of food stacked ridiculously high.

'What?' she replied.

'You laughed.'

Brooke pulled her face. 'I did not.'

'You did,' Sierra said, giving her a sympathetic look.

'I did *not*,' she said, although at this point she was fairly certain she had. She looked at her nephew. 'Did I, Marcus?'

Her nephew nodded solemnly.

She sighed. 'Only four years old and already turning against his aunt.'

But she winked at him, and he offered her a bright smile. She snorted when she saw the potato in his mouth, then sobered quickly when his mother reprimanded him.

'So, are you going to tell us?' Dom asked.

'No.'

Dom paused before he took a bite of his own potato. 'No?'

'No.'

'You're acting weird.' He lowered his fork. 'Come to think of it, you've been acting weird since you arrived.'

'It's seeing your new haircut,' she replied, even as a ripple of unease went through her. 'That fade is not a good look for you.'

Her brother looked as if he wanted to swear at her, but his eyes settled on his son and he merely said, 'You're lying.'

'I am,' she agreed. 'Which should tell you how unwilling I am to talk about whatever it is making me act weird.'

They stared at one another. Brooke held his gaze because she knew that if she didn't, it would look as if she was hiding something. She wasn't. Yes, there was the small matter of wanting to move on with her life, but there was nothing wrong with that. Right? Wasn't that what she'd told Tyler? That wanting a life where she was important, too, wasn't a bad thing?

Except it had been easier to tell him that than to believe it herself. She didn't know how to feel about moving on sometimes. Especially in this circumstance. Was it because things with her and Tyler were different from how things with her and Kian had been? Or was it because she felt as if she was betraying her husband by wanting someone else? Was it guilt because the only reason she *could* want someone else was because her husband had died?

She should make an appointment with her therapist, but she already knew what he would say. It was probably all of it.

They'd already established that she wanted to live her life for Kian. To move forward because he couldn't. For the most part she was succeeding. She was doing well at work, her relationship with her family was strong. It was really only moving on romantically that was the problem.

And knowing that didn't change anything one bit.

'Brooke—'

'Sierra,' Brooke said, ignoring her brother and whatever that placating tone of voice was about to bring, 'how's work going?'

Sierra's eyes shifted between Dom and Brooke,

but she answered Brooke's question, as if realising it would be safer than whatever Dom had been about to ask. The conversation moved from there to Brooke's work, and the fact that she was nearing the end of a project pretty soon.

'Another week, maybe a few more days, and we'll be done.'

'Days before deadline, too,' Dom said, and there was pride in his voice even though this was the first time he'd spoken since she'd brushed him off.

'Yep. Hopefully that'll mean the launch will go smoothly.'

'Do you still want me to come with you?'

'Oh.'

She'd forgotten she'd told Dom she wanted him to come. It had felt like a significant event, one she didn't want to deal with alone. But between when she'd asked him and now she hadn't thought about it again.

She warned her brain not to point out any helpful reasons as to why.

'Yeah, I'd love that,' she said.

'You sure?' Sierra teased. 'You hesitated for a bit. Is there someone else you'd rather take?'

It was teasing. Simple teasing. And if she'd brushed it off, called it ridiculous, they would have laughed and moved on.

Except she didn't.

She opened her mouth. Closed it. Like a fish at the water's surface, eating its food. Only she wasn't doing something sensible like eating or, say, defending herself. She was revealing something she'd rather not have anyone know. Not now, when it was messy and complicated. Maybe not ever.

And then—*then*—she did the next worst thing. She blushed. A blood rushing to her face, heat exploding in her cheeks blush.

'Oh…' Sierra said slowly, her mouth forming the letter, too. 'Oh, Brooke. I'm so, so sorry.'

Brooke looked at Sierra. Sympathised. At least she would have if she hadn't been the one in the line of fire. Because the reason Sierra was apologising wasn't because she'd teased Brooke, but because of the reaction such a revelation was going to elicit from Dom.

'She's right?' Dom asked, his gaze intense. 'There's someone in your life?'

She took a second to reply, aware that her physical reaction had already revealed a lot.

'I have many people in my life,' she said slowly.

'Brooke,' her brother said with a patience she knew he didn't feel, 'do you have someone *romantic* in your life?'

'Well, considering how you treat Sierra, I think you're romantic. Does that—?'

'Brooke.'

It was a bark now. She winced.

'There might be someone. But honestly,' she rushed to say, not allowing him to interrupt, 'it's nothing.'

'Who is he?'

'Who said it was a he?'

'Brooke.'

'Dom,' she deadpanned. 'You realise I am thirty years old? An adult?' She spelled it out for him. 'I do not have to justify my actions or my decisions to you. I am not a kid, nor am I a suspect you can interrogate simply because you want to.'

The silence that followed was long and tense. Brooke stared at Dom; Dom stared right back.

When it dipped into ridiculous territory, Sierra spoke. 'Hey, Marcus, we're just about done here. How about you and I take dessert…?' She trailed off, as if realising she hadn't exactly thought it through, then said, 'Literally anywhere other than here!'

Marcus eyed Brooke and Dom, but silently slipped off his chair and followed his mom into another room.

As soon as they'd left, Dom leaned forward. 'That's unfair and you know it.'

'Maybe,' said Brooke, 'but so is making me feel like I'm doing something irresponsible.'

'I never once said—' He broke off at the look she gave him. 'All right, fine. I might be giving off that vibe. But it's not because I don't trust you to make good decisions for yourself.'

'Really? Because it sure sounds like it.'

'I don't trust other people,' he said. 'And I know you're about to tell me that's a cliché, but it's literally my job to be suspicious. Is it so wrong for me to be protective of my sister? My sister who's lost too much in her life and deserves happiness?'

Her heart softened, which she knew had been his intention, and she narrowed her eyes. 'I know what you're doing.'

He gave her a twist of a smile. 'Is it working?'

'You know it is.'

His smile widened. There was a slight pause before he said, 'Are you happy?'

She sat back in her chair. 'What does it mean that I don't know how to answer that?'

'You should be happy,' he replied carefully. 'But I think it'll be hard for you to figure out because you don't know what that means any more. At least not when it comes to romance.'

She blinked. 'That's surprisingly astute, Dom.'

'I've been married for ten years.'

'I thought most of that success was Sierra's doing.' But she smiled at him before she sobered. 'It's true.' She paused. 'I don't know. I don't know if what I'm feeling is what I'm supposed to be feeling. It feels like too much, too soon.'

'The relationship? Or the fact that it's happening at all?'

'It's been five years,' she answered, though it wasn't really an answer. At least, not a truthful answer.

The truth was that sometimes it felt like either one of those. Sometimes both—sometimes neither. But she couldn't tell her brother that. She would sound unstable. She *felt* unstable.

'I want it to feel normal,' she admitted. 'I want it to be easy and normal and… I don't know… I don't want to feel like I'm coming into this relationship with some kind of internal deficit. That's how I feel right now.'

'Like your grief is a deficit?'

'Baggage,' she said with a nod. 'Why would anyone want that?'

Dom took a while to answer. 'Everyone has baggage. This guy—or whatever this person's gender,' he added, 'will have it, too. Sure, it might not be grief, but it'll be something. No baggage is equal in a relationship, but that's probably what makes it equal.'

'That makes no sense,' she teased.

'Yeah, I know.'

'It's still pretty wise, though.'

'I know that, too.'

She laughed.

They sat in silence again, but it was easy this

time. It made her nostalgic for the days when they were growing up. They would fight as though they had everything to lose, even when the fight was over something idiotic like the remote control. An hour or so later they'd be sitting together on the couch, watching a show and arguing without heat over something as idiotic as the topic of their original fight.

'There's no such thing as normal,' Dom said gently.

He reached out to take her hand, and the comfort of having her big brother holding her hand soothed the uncertainty in her heart.

'We pretend like there is, but there isn't. There's only what works for us. So if this person works for you, B, that's enough. You don't have to have all the answers now.'

She smiled at him, thanked him, and then went to tell Sierra it was safe for her and Marcus to come back to the kitchen. Brooke and Dom made a special effort to show Marcus they were getting along, so he knew that their tiff had been a simple one.

'It's time you got him a sibling,' she told Dom when she left. 'He needs to know that family fights aren't the end of the world.'

'Your wish is our command.'

'That's a weird— Wait,' she said, when she

took in his smile. 'Sierra's pregnant? You're having another kid?'

'In seven more months, yeah.'

She squealed, jumped into her brother's arms, and then went back inside to tell her sister-in-law that she was excited and would be there for her no matter what.

The happiness of the news followed her as she drove home. It coated her thoughts, so that they felt happy even though she was still thinking about what Dom had said.

Did Tyler work for her? There were certainly moments. Those moments happened when they were together. It was the distance between them that was filled with uncertainty.

But that wasn't what stayed with her the most. What struck her the most was Dom saying she didn't have to have all the answers now. Under normal circumstances, she would have agreed. Except with Tyler it felt as if there was an element of urgency. A time limit if he was leaving. And he wanted to leave, so the fact that he would seemed almost inevitable.

If distance was what caused uncertainty, there was no hope for a long-distance relationship.

So yeah, she did kind of feel that she needed to figure out all the answers now.

When she got home, she found Tyler sitting on her front step.

'I didn't mean *right* now. Like at this moment,' she muttered under her breath as she got out of the car. 'What are you doing here? No—wait,' she said as she stopped in front of him. 'That was rude. Hello, Tyler. What brings you here?'

He gave her a half-smile she didn't feel was completely sincere.

'Was that better?' she asked.

'Six out of ten.'

'A pass.' She wanted to smile at him, but his expression didn't encourage that. 'So, are you going to tell me?'

'I… Do you mind if we go somewhere?'

'Somewhere?'

'There's a vineyard a little way from here.'

'Wine? Are you trying to soften me up?'

'Would it work if I was?'

He was teasing, but something in his voice made him sound serious. And curious.

She angled her head. 'Yeah. Sure. Should I drive with you? Or…?'

'You can drive with me.'

'Lead the way.'

He did. And, after the slightest moment of hesitation, she followed.

Tyler knew she was picking up on how strangely he was acting. He wasn't particularly proud of it, but a sense of inevitability had woven a spell over him. A dark, disruptive spell that wouldn't allow him to continue his life without having this conversation with her.

He'd spent a week going over it in his head. Did he tell her the truth? That they'd met before or shortly after her husband's death? It would be a hell of a thing for her to find out, and that was part of why he needed to figure out whether he should tell her. How would she respond? Would it bring anything good?

But he couldn't sit on the information. The only reason he had before was because he'd thought she had chosen not to acknowledge their shared past. Hell, at this point, he didn't even know if he could call it 'shared.' Could he still think that it happened to both of them if she didn't remember it? And what did he tell her about it?

It had been a week of dinners and friendship, including going to the vineyard he was taking her to now—a sneaky attempt at jogging her memory, especially because he knew it was pointless.

If she was going to remember their time together, it would have happened already. He didn't understand the science behind memory loss, despite the hours of research he'd done, but from what Brooke had told him it was her trauma. Which meant it was designed to protect her. Not much could change that. He didn't want anything to change that.

So maybe the reason he was taking her to this place was more for him. To assure himself that something *had* happened between them.

It was all so messy.

'What's wrong?' Brooke asked as he took the curved road leading to the vineyard.

It was one of many vineyards in the area, with fields of green and gold stretching out for metres and metres around them. On another day, he would have taken the time to enjoy the view. The way the sun hit the leaves, casting light, making the colours seem as if they were glowing. The mountains in the distance, all curves and angles of darkness balancing the expanse of green.

It was one of his favourite drives, especially as they got closer to the vineyard, when trees reached over the road, shadowing the cars beneath them. When a burst of sun trickled through the gaps of the leaves, or through the stretches without trees, or when the fields and mountains were once again unobscured.

But he couldn't enjoy it today. Only he didn't want her to know that.

'Why would you think anything's wrong?' he asked.

He glanced over to see her arch her brow, as if to say, *Which example would you like? The one where you show up at my house unannounced after a week of no communication? Or the one where you ask to take me to a vineyard without telling me why? Or your general current broodiness?*

As a gift to both of them, she merely said, 'You were shaking your head.'

'I was…thinking.' He stuck his tongue into his cheek, ashamed of how inadequate that was.

'Okay.'

He looked at her again, but she was looking out of the window, so he couldn't see her expression. He didn't need to see it to know she was giving him an out. She had been since the moment she'd got home. She hadn't questioned him too much, wasn't pushing him when it was clear that he didn't want to talk about something.

It wouldn't last, so for now, he enjoyed it. Or, since enjoyment wasn't something he could feel at this moment, with tension skittering over his skin like a ghost, he accepted it.

The rest of the drive was quiet, and when he pulled into the car park he got out, waited for her to join him, and then took the short stone path to the front of the restaurant. He helped her up the steps.

When she gasped, he gave her some space to enjoy the view. He hadn't intended for it to be this way, but the sun was lowering beneath the fields in the distance, and the patio they were standing on allowed them a perfect view of it.

It was breathtaking, truly, but his attention

was on Brooke. The sun made her look like an ethereal being who had come down from heaven to give him an impossible task. He would have readily accepted it, he knew.

How could he resist that golden-brown skin, shimmering like the grains of sand at a beach? Or the pink of her cheeks, her lips, a hue he had only ever seen on the most tempting of fruit? Or her eyes, the brown lighter than ever under the sun, that looked as though she were ready to give away every secret? Or perhaps as though she could keep such secrets. The deepest, darkest kind. The sweetest kind.

He didn't realise he was closing the distance between them until he had. When he was there, his hand lifted. She shifted just as a breeze floated over them, mingling her scent with the spicy sweet smell of the wine, with the grounded smell of the earth around them. Her shift wasn't to move away. Even though her eyes traced the movement of his hand as he tucked some strands of her hair behind her ear, she didn't move away.

She leaned in.

It undid him in ways he couldn't explain, hadn't expected, and his head was dipping to hers before he could talk himself out of it. She met him halfway, her lips soft and ready, as though made for his kiss.

The kiss was neither firm nor gentle; not intense nor easy. It was simply a kiss. An acknowledgement of their attraction and of the *more* that haunted each of them.

He cupped her face. Opened his mouth. Swept his tongue inside to taste her. It was a taste that would mark him for ever. An exaggeration, perhaps, though his senses didn't seem to think so. It reminded him of the sun during early spring, of cold water after a hot summer's day, of a fire during the frigid cold.

Her touch was both foreign and familiar. Even now, with her fingers hesitantly touching his torso. And seconds later, when they curled into his shirt, bringing him closer to her with a strength he didn't resist.

His body was aware of her every motion, as if she were tracing his skin with a block of ice. Desire sent pulses to every pleasure-point in his body, and he shifted, sliding his arms around her waist, pulling her closer so that when they parted, no one would see the evidence of what she did to him.

Then he realised that he was allowing her to feel what she did to him. He angled himself, trying to give her space. His body complained. So did she. And with that came another shift of her body, moving the softness of her against the hardness of him.

He was terribly aware of her breasts pressing

against his chest. His fingers ached to trace them. His eyes wanted to feast on them. To memorise their colour and shape and curve, every mark on her skin. And when he was done looking he wanted to taste. Run his tongue over every point. Lick the marks to celebrate their uniqueness.

And when he was done there he would move on to the rest of her body. To her waist that sloped over hips that were plush and ready for lifting. She would wrap her legs around him and give him better access to her heat. He would finally give the hardness between his legs what it was asking for. What it was demanding.

'Whoa,' she breathed as she pulled away.

For a second he wondered if she had some idea of what he'd been thinking. If she was scandalised or agreeing to what he wanted to do to her.

Then she said, 'That was a…a hell of a kiss.'

She exhaled, the air rushing through her lips and touching his face. It did nothing to ease his arousal. Only heightened it, reminding him of what she tasted like.

He took his own steadying breath. A couple more. Eventually, he said, 'Yeah.'

Her tongue slid to the corner of her mouth. There was an amused look on her face. 'I've rendered you speechless. I quite like that power.'

'By now you should already know you have it.'

'No,' she disagreed. 'By now I know that no

matter what I say, you'll always have the perfect response. It'll be charming and very annoying and I'll still feel a part of me...' She trailed off, the teasing tone of her voice disappearing. 'Soften,' she finished.

If his body had been all in with that kiss, now it was his heart's chance. Her words sank into it like rain into fertile soil. It was too early to tell what would grow from that soil, if anything. Because the moment he told her the truth, it would yank out the root, and any hope that something beautiful and full of life would come from it would be gone.

'I have to tell you something,' he said, stepping away from her. Leaving the heat and the desire in that little space where they'd kissed.

Her eyes became unreadable, and she stepped out of the space, too. He spent a moment too long staring at it, wondering if what they'd left there was simpler or more complicated than what they were about to enter into.

'What?' she asked carefully.

With a fortifying breath, he said, 'We've met before.'

CHAPTER THIRTEEN

BROOKE COULD TELL by the tone of his voice that he wasn't talking about a random meeting. She couldn't remember it. And, although it was true she didn't remember many men from the time when she was with Kian, she was certain she would have remembered Tyler. He was striking to look at, and she would have at least made that distant connection, even when she was in a relationship.

A ripple of unease went through her body, rolling over her skin much as the breeze did.

'Okay, so, you've brought me to a vineyard with a beautiful view and a stunning restaurant—' she assumed it was stunning since she hadn't really taken a good look inside the building and doubted she would now '—to tell me... what? We've met once before?'

'It wasn't just once.'

She felt the impact of those words physically.

'We know—*knew*—one another.'

'I... I don't understand.' He opened his mouth

to explain, but she held up a hand. 'And if I'm going to understand, I think I'm going to need wine. Which, I assume, is at least part of why you brought me here?'

His expression was sombre as he nodded, gesturing for her to walk in front of him.

It was hard for her to imagine that this was the same man who'd kissed her so thoroughly only a few minutes ago. She had thrown caution to the wind—hell, she'd been swept away by that wind—and kissed him in public because the look he had given her had been so damn intimate. And trusting. She couldn't forget that. It had triggered something inside her. He trusted her and, yes, she trusted him.

So, she'd kissed him. Let him touch her soul with the lick of his tongue and the caress of his fingers.

Now she felt as though she were about to lose it all.

The thought distracted her from really noticing the restaurant, though she knew it was gorgeous. The wall facing the vineyard was made from glass and metal panels, the space above it decorated in an intricate white pattern. But all she could do when they were seated in a secluded section of the room was stare at the menu.

She chose a wine with a high alcohol content. Didn't speak until that wine was brought for her approval. In truth, she didn't taste it. But she pretended to, so that the waiter would leave.

When he was gone, she drank the entire glass. With a nod, she told Tyler, 'I'm ready.'

He had been silent since they'd left the balcony. The crinkle around his eyes, the purse of his lips, told her it was nerves. An echo of the same thing danced in her chest, her stomach. She soothed it with deep breaths, in and out, and tried to focus on that and not on the signs of Tyler's nerves.

It was about fifty per cent effective, and then, when he began to talk, it stopped working entirely.

'We met on the tenth of July five years ago. I was at the hospital to see my sister. She had just given birth to her son. And I needed...' He shook his head. 'Well, I found you in the coffee shop around the corner when I went to get something to drink.'

The tenth of July... That was the day she'd signed Kian's DNR. She knew that. The accident had happened on the evening of the second, Kian had been in the hospital until he'd died on the tenth, the funeral had been on the seventeenth.

Her first real memories of that time started at some point after that.

Tyler was waiting, as if he'd known that she would need time to get it all straight in her head. The fact that he had given her dates supported that.

Nausea welled, and suddenly she wished she hadn't drunk the wine at all.

'What…what happened?' she asked hoarsely.

'You looked like you'd had a rough evening. I thought I could help with that.' He shrugged, as if the logic of that seemed shaky to him now. 'I asked you if you wanted to have your coffee at my table and you agreed.'

'We had *coffee*?'

'Yes.'

'The night Kian died I had *coffee* with a *stranger*?'

Again, it felt as if the news had physically hit her.

She sat back, tried to remember what Dom had told her about that night. He'd wanted to take her home, but she hadn't been ready to leave. She'd insisted on staying. She'd wanted space. And because her family was so supportive, so understanding, they'd given it to her.

She had always assumed she had gone home. Mourned and grieved like everyone had expected her to. But no. Apparently, she had gone out for coffee.

'I'm sorry,' said Tyler.

Her eyes flickered up. 'You didn't know about any of it.'

'You believe me?'

'Why would you lie about this, Tyler?' She asked the question with a hopeless kind of despair. It would have troubled her at another time, but for the moment it was appropriate. 'Apart from the fairly obvious fact that we've known one another for over a month now and you haven't mentioned any of this before.'

He winced. 'I thought you weren't mentioning it intentionally. I was about to work for you. You seemed to be all about boundaries, so I was, too. I didn't want to push for the sake of Tia's job, but also because I thought—' He broke off with a sharp exhalation. 'I thought wrong, clearly.'

'Knowing what you know about me now,' she said slowly, 'like the fact that I can't keep a secret to save my life, you thought I wouldn't mention going out for coffee with you?' She snorted, though she knew it was an ugly thing to do. 'Did we not have a good time? Did I give you some kind of sign that I'd pretend it had never happened if we ever met again?'

Colour entered his face. It was a charming red, something that belonged among fields of flowers, and she would have found it charming if it hadn't been so alarming. It was an indication that she was missing something—which, yes, obviously—and something significant.

'What?' She almost hissed. 'What happened? Oh, no, ' she said, rearing back. 'Did I...? Did we...?'

'No! Well, we didn't... We didn't sleep together.'

'But something else happened?'

A curt nod. 'We kissed.'

Good heavens.

She reached for her wine glass before realising it hadn't been refilled. Desperately, she looked around for the server. Didn't see him. Unhelpfully, her mind told her that she had just regretted drinking the first glass of wine. A second would likely have similar consequences. And yet she still desperately wanted to drink. To fill the sudden void that came with the knowledge that she had kissed someone the night her husband had died.

What kind of person did that make her? Certainly not the one she had always thought she was. Not the woman who had, for the last five years, been living a pious life of offering to her deceased husband.

She hadn't thought about it that way, of course. But now it seemed obvious that she had been. Only she hadn't realised it was in atonement for her sins.

'Right,' she said after a moment, taking a deep breath. 'You and I kissed. Okay. Sure. That's fine.

I mean, I'd only been single—and I use that term really lightly, because *wow* it messes with my brain—for literal hours.'

Again, colour appeared on his skin. It wasn't embarrassment though. She knew it deep in her gut—a feeling that had nebulous implications now she knew they had some sort of history together. No, it was distress. He didn't want to tell her any of this.

If she hadn't trusted him, she would have thought that was why he'd waited so long before he'd said anything. But there was still something inside her that *did* trust him, despite this earthquake to the foundations she'd thought they'd built. And the same gut feeling told her that the distress wasn't for himself either, but for her. He didn't want to upset her.

'What?' she asked flatly. 'Please, tell me. I don't think... I think these little bursts of shock are worse than you laying it all out for me. So just...just tell me.'

He nodded. 'The kiss didn't happen the night your husband died. It was a week after. We saw one another every day for dinner in the days leading up to...it. For that whole week.' Though he looked uncomfortable, he didn't shift. 'We'd look up places the day before and meet there the next evening. We didn't have each other's numbers. We knew one another's names, but that was the only personal information we shared. Mostly we spoke about random but meaningful things. Or we made the kind of ridiculous observations that you'd only feel comfortable making with a stranger.'

He paused. She wasn't sure if it was to take a breath or to give her a moment to process. If it were the latter, she should tell him not to bother. She currently only had the mental space to receive information. Understanding that information, emotionally or mentally, would require energy and a presence of mind that she didn't have.

So she waited. And when it became clear that she wasn't going to speak—it seemed he *had* been waiting for her to process—he continued.

'It was a good week. For me,' he clarified. 'I thought for you, too. Especially when we...' the slightest hesitation '...kissed. Hell, that's why the kiss happened. But then you disappeared. I didn't see you again until a month ago. And I thought—'

'You thought I hadn't felt what you felt,' she said, seeing it now. 'You thought I was ignoring everything that had happened between us because I didn't feel the same way. That's why you didn't say anything.'

He sucked in his bottom lip, but nodded. 'And then last week, when you told me you had amnesia, I realised... I realised it wasn't a choice.'

'And that it had nothing to do with you or your ego.' Abruptly, she pushed her chair back. His eyes widened, but she was walking away before he could say anything. Before her mind could catch up with what her body was doing.

'Brooke!'

He called after her, but she didn't respond. Only kept walking. Likely because some part of her knew that he would have to stay behind, sort out the bill. It wouldn't give her hours—in hindsight, she should have come with her own car—but it would give her enough time to figure out how her lungs worked again.

She rushed down the stairs, clutching at the railing when she almost fell on the last two steps, then walked towards the vineyard, metres from the building. When she reached the entrance, she ran. Not her smartest idea, considering she was wearing a white dress and sandals. But she didn't care about calling herself smart when she was only trying to survive the onslaught of feelings Tyler's words had awoken in her.

She'd described it as an earthquake before, but that had been in terms of them. That wasn't the only thing his revelation had affected. It was an earthquake for all the emotions she'd thought she'd worked through since Kian's death. If she looked at them now, it seemed she had merely been stacking them neatly, and now, with this earthquake, they were falling over. Coming to crush her, really, like an avalanche rushing down a hill. And, like any person on that hill, she had no hope of dodging it, only delaying it.

She could only delay it for so long.

She dropped to her knees, not caring that dirt caked the material of her dress. The only thing she cared about was the fact that she was far enough away from the restaurant that no one would see her unless they were standing on the balcony. And if her own actions on that balcony were anything to go by, whoever stood there now wouldn't be paying attention to a sobbing woman crouching in the dirt.

Sobbing? She lifted her hand and realised that there were, indeed, tears coming down her face. But her lungs were working again, which surely was a good sign. So what if her breathing wasn't optimal? So what if that rush of in-out, in-out meant panic and anxiety and not normal, functioning human organs?

'Brooke.'

She groaned, sitting back on the ground and bringing her knees up so she could hide her face in between them.

'Do you…do you want me to go?'

'What would make you think that? The fact that I literally ran away from you? Or the fact that I'm crying in the middle of a field of grapes?'

She said all those words between inhalations and exhalations of air, between splutters and hiccups, and all from between her knees. So when she felt Tyler sit down next to her, she thought she might not have delivered the words as concisely and as sharply as she'd intended to.

'I figure whatever you're saying means yes, you'd like me to go.'

Perhaps she *had* delivered the words that way.

'And I will,' he continued, 'as soon as I'm sure you won't get killed out here in the middle of nowhere.'

'Killed?' she repeated, lifting her head. 'Really?'

He shrugged, but his eyes were soft. 'I wanted to say as soon as I'm sure you're okay, but I didn't think you'd be receptive to that.'

'But I'd be receptive to the prospect of murder?'

'You're not crying any more.'

She did a mental check, and of course, he was right. She sucked in her lips and rested her chin on her knees. Then she turned her head and rested her cheek there instead. It was more comfortable. It also had the added benefit of allowing her not to look at Tyler.

To his credit, he didn't bother her. Apart from with his presence, which always had some kind of an effect on her. That attraction, the electricity…

She hated it now. Hated the overwhelming awareness that he was here and Kian was not.

She shut her eyes, but the thought had already
brought more tears. Silent, thankfully. In fact,
it was much less dramatic than running into a
field and sobbing. But her hysteria had hidden
the deepest factor in all of this. The thing that
had caused the drama, ironically.

The betrayal. Because heaven—and likely
Kian—knew that she had betrayed him.

And she couldn't remember it.

She wanted to call her psychologist and ask
whether that made it better or worse. Maybe it
was the reason for her memory loss. That kind
of betrayal would have been deeply traumatic
to her, especially if her husband had just died.

She could already hear her psychologist's
voice, pointing out how she had had both physical and emotional trauma, and that both of those
things were already adequate explanations. But
how did that account for her actions after Kian's death? Hadn't she remembered the accident
and everything else then? Dom had told her
she'd handled everything in a daze, but she'd
handled it.

Someone who didn't remember her husband,
who didn't know what she was doing, wouldn't
have done that.

Did that mean she'd remembered Kian but

started dating a stranger? Had it been some kind of grieving process?

Even the idea of it was abhorrent to her. She hadn't dated in five years as part of her grieving process. Falling for someone immediately after Kian's death didn't seem likely.

So what had happened?

Slowly, she turned her head to Tyler. He wasn't looking at her. He was affording her as much privacy as he could, apparently. He must have sensed that she was looking at him though, because he turned then, holding her eyes.

And even in that moment, even in her turmoil, she felt it. A gentle tug in the pit of her belly, a fluttering in the region of her heart. It was awareness, and attraction, but neither felt dirty nor shameful, though in the circumstances, both should have.

Maybe this was it. This was the reason she had agreed to have coffee with him. There was a pull between them that defied logic and circumstance. Something that had nothing to do with choice or agency. Something inevitable.

She wanted to ask him questions, to find out the nature of the relationship that had led to that kiss. But all she could do was shut her eyes and press them into her knees.

Because she had just realised she was in love with him, and it was a hell of a time for that.

* * *

'You're not supposed to be here. Nyle is still sick and—'

'Tia,' Tyler interrupted.

He didn't intend it to come out as a plea, but he couldn't think of any other intention when he actually heard his own tone of voice.

Leaning into it, he added, 'Please.'

Tia's eyes swept over his face, then she stepped outside. 'Nyle's sleeping at the moment, but I'm not sure how long that'll last. He's feeling better, and apparently I've gone back to having a ninja in training in my house.'

'A ninja in training?' His mouth curved, despite the rawness that had had him driving to his sister's house after dropping Brooke at home. 'Your words or his?'

'His,' she replied dryly. 'Once we get through this, I'll have to talk to him about putting limitations on his dreams. He could be a ninja, not just one in training.'

'At least he's being realistic.'

'He's five. I'm not sure that's the lesson I want to teach the kid.'

'That's why you're such a great mom.'

Her eyes narrowed a fraction. 'Your face looks like you've witnessed a murder *and* you're complimenting me? Something must be wrong.'

He didn't bother to answer, only sank down

in front of the door. It meant he was sitting directly on the pathway that led to the door from the garage.

Tia lived in the house their mother had bought once the divorce from their father had been finalised. She hadn't paid off the mortgage before her death, but Tyler had taken care of that, and when Nyle had arrived, he'd signed his share of the house over for his nephew to inherit when he was old enough. It had been the only help Tia had accepted, and he was fairly certain the only reason she had was because she had still been grieving their mother.

He could remember the days when he'd come out the house to see his mother struggling with groceries. She would never call for him, and he would always ask why she hadn't. Her answer would be a look. A look said, *I can do this by myself.* And, sure, she could—but she hadn't had to. That had been his mother's greatest flaw, and it was one Tia seemed to have inherited.

He hadn't though. When he'd dropped Brooke off and she'd left the car with only a murmur of thanks, he'd known he needed someone. And the only person he had was Tia.

That was why he couldn't leave. Certainly not for the other side of the world. But he couldn't handle thinking about that now. He'd deal with it later. Right now, he was panicking about something entirely different.

'Let me guess,' Tia said, lowering herself down next to him. 'This is about our boss.'

His head whipped towards her. 'How did you know? Also—*our*?'

'Technically, she's my boss, but in reality she's yours. Besides, she texted me to ask for your number. Did you not think I'd put two and two together?'

'You *were* suspiciously quiet about that.'

'I was dealing with a sick kid.'

'When has that ever stopped you?'

'Maybe I knew that you'd pitch up at my door, desperate for my guidance.'

She wasn't being entirely snarky—although with Tia, that was always a factor. There was also a sincerity that made him wonder what she'd seen to make her respond this way.

'Am I that bad at relationships?' he asked.

'I don't know,' she answered honestly. 'That's why I expected you to come to me. Not because I'm in any way an expert at relationships, as you well know, but because...' She looked out at the road in front of them where a couple of kids were kicking a ball back and forth. 'When you need advice, you ask. It's one of the things I admire most about you.'

He didn't give himself time to enjoy his surprise. 'Go on.'

She stuck her tongue out. 'If you had any real friends, you'd probably go to them—'

'Ah, *there* it is. I knew the compliments wouldn't last.'

'But the people you call friends are mostly colleagues and you wouldn't go to any of them about something you consider personal.'

She wasn't wrong.

'And since Mom has died, that leaves me. So, how can I help?'

'After everything you've just said, I shouldn't want your help.'

'But you need it.'

He sighed. He did need it. So he told her everything, from the moment he'd seen Brooke in that coffee shop. He didn't stop until he reached today. He left out anything physical—he didn't need his little sister knowing about that—as well as Brooke crying in the middle of the vineyard.

He wasn't sure why, but that felt as if it were a secret. His or hers, he didn't know. But it felt precious that he'd seen her so raw, so vulnerable, and he couldn't bear the idea of sharing that moment with anyone else.

It didn't even matter that seeing her had broken his heart. Had made him want to build a wall around her so she never had to face anything that would upset her so much again. Even him. He considered it a privilege that she'd been so open with him and he wouldn't do anything to betray that trust.

So he merely ended by telling Tia that Brooke had been upset. That he had been, too, and that was why he was there.

'I'm sorry,' Tia said, curling her fingers around his. 'I'm sorry you're sad and I'm sorry that this relationship is so complicated. You don't deserve it.'

'Don't I?' he asked bitterly.

'You don't. You helped Mom take care of us. You took care of me. You still help me and Nyle.' She squeezed his hand. 'You deserve only good things, Tyler. You've spent a lifetime earning good karma.'

Maybe I've cancelled it out these last few months. By wanting to expand my business and to leave you and Nyle to fend for yourselves. I want it more every time I think of it. Despite knowing what Dad did. Despite not wanting to put myself first like he did, I'm still considering it.

It would have been so easy to say it. To finally be honest. But, coward that he was, he didn't. He only squeezed her hand back and allowed himself to lie, telling himself it was because he was focusing on one disaster at a time.

'It doesn't matter,' he said. 'This job will be over in a week and it won't be a problem any more.'

'Won't it?' Tia asked lightly. 'Since when does running away from your problems make them any easier to deal with? I'm asking that sincerely,' she added, 'because I've been running for five years, yet I still think about the lying piece of crap that gave me the most beautiful gift in the world.'

He softened. 'It's *because* he gave you that gift.'

'No,' she denied. 'It's because there's still a part of me that loves him. And you don't have to say it. I know I'm an idiot.'

'I've spent five years comparing anyone I was even remotely interested in to a woman I didn't see again after she literally ran away from our kiss. I'm the last person to judge.'

They fell into silence. He didn't know what Tia was thinking about, but he was thinking about all the mistakes he'd made since he'd been reunited with Brooke. If he'd maintained a professional relationship with her...if he'd been honest with her upfront...if he'd asked her why she'd run after their kiss...

There had been so many opportunities to alter where they had ended up now, only he had been too in love to take them.

He should be surprised by that revelation, but he wasn't. The feeling had been there for longer than he'd realised. He'd been like a frog in heating water, not realising he was being boiled until it was too late to escape. But even if he had realised it, he wasn't certain he would have escaped. He had enjoyed that heating water too much, just like he'd enjoyed the falling.

Spending time with Brooke. Getting to know her mind, her humour, her heart. He wouldn't have sacrificed that even to save himself from the inevitable heartbreak. Because it would be inevitable. They had no future. They couldn't when their past together was an obstacle between them. When her past would keep her from moving forward.

He didn't resent it. It was a part of her life and he didn't want her to ignore it for the sake of his comfort. Especially not when he had his own past to consider. His own obstacles.

What would happen if he left South Africa? If by some miracle he actually went to London and worked towards his dreams? Would he leave Brooke behind? Would he leave a woman he loved behind? How could he claim to be better than his father if he did that?

'What do you want, Tyler?' Tia asked, interrupting his thoughts. 'In an ideal world, what would you want?'

'Her,' he answered honestly, despite all the reasons he'd told himself he couldn't have her. 'I'd want a life with her. She's smart and funny. Sweet.' He smiled, thinking about her and Mochi. 'She has a dog she thinks hates her because she can't give him the love he deserves, even though it's clear he adores her and she gives him more love than she knows. She works hard. She has this special project she's working on and she loves her job. And...' He trailed off, his mind finally catching up to his mouth. 'But I can't have her.'

'Because she doesn't feel the same way?'

'Because we have too many obstacles in the way of being happy together.'

His sister was quiet for a while. 'Seems to me that if you feel the way you do, and she feels that way, too, the biggest obstacle is already out of the way. The first and most logical step now would be to figure out if she thinks *you're* smart and funny and sweet and all those other things. Doubtful, but you've got to try.'

She bumped his shoulder to show she was teasing. He already knew that. What he couldn't fathom was why her advice made him feel better. Even if Brooke did feel the same way, he'd just told himself why it didn't matter. So why did it feel so urgent to know?

'You're a lot smarter than I give you credit for, do you know that?' he told Tia.

'I do,' she said with a smirk, but sobered quickly. 'You can't make decisions when you don't know the facts. She can't figure out if she wants to be with you if you don't tell her that you want to be with her.'

'You're right.' And Tia deserved to know all the facts, too. He took a huge breath. 'T, that's not the only thing I want to talk about...'

And finally, after months of stalling, he told his sister the truth.

CHAPTER FOURTEEN

'You're acting weird,' Dom pointed out unhelpfully.

'It's the launch of my app,' Brooke snapped. 'What's normal in these circumstances?'

'Not snapping at your brother for making a simple observation.'

She didn't reply, but stuck out her tongue. The action held the same tone as whatever she might have told him anyway.

Thankfully, he didn't respond, verbally or physically. It was as if, for once in his life, Dom knew she didn't need his snide comments.

She was highly strung, without a doubt. She had been since that conversation with Tyler. She'd been going back and forth about what it meant and how she felt in every spare moment she had.

Those moments had been rare, fortunately, because the final week before the launch of the app had been busy. And tonight, they would officially go live.

As was the custom for her company, they'd

planned a black-tie event to watch the clock tick down and celebrate the exact moment. Dom had pitched up in his tuxedo when she'd asked him to, which had also annoyed her for some inexplicable reason. Even though he'd picked Mochi up earlier, to stay with him and Sierra for the night.

But none of that meant she was acting weird, regardless of what he'd said.

The doorbell rang. She looked at the clock. 'That can't be the driver yet. There's still thirty minutes before the car's meant to arrive.'

'And yet you asked me to be here thirty minutes ago,' Dom muttered.

'I didn't want to risk being late.'

He merely grunted, which was an appropriate response to her lie. She hadn't only wanted to avoid being late. She'd wanted to celebrate with her brother. Yet the unopened bottle of very expensive champagne she'd bought at the start of the process still stood in her refrigerator, untouched.

She couldn't bring herself to celebrate. It didn't feel right when there was so much that felt wrong in her life.

For example, the fact that you don't really want Dom here, but Tyler.

Irritably, she stomped over to the front door and yanked it open.

And stared.

She might have been ashamed if Tyler hadn't been staring at her, too.

She thought it might both have come from shock, although their reasons might be different. For her, it was simply his presence. Had she somehow manifested him? She didn't even care, too distracted by a strong wave of pleasure that hit her at seeing him again.

His expression was sombre, those beautiful lines of his face arranged in a serious expression she wasn't used to seeing. But he was still heart-achingly handsome. He wore a simple shirt and jeans, and her fingers itched to touch him. It felt like such a long time ago that they'd shared those kisses, but she remembered them so vividly.

And all of it felt like a terrible irony considering she couldn't remember the time he claimed they'd spent together.

No, not claimed—the time they *had* spent together.

She was pretty certain it had happened. There was no benefit to him in lying about it. And it made sense, though it had taken her long to admit it. It explained how she'd felt such a bond with him only shortly after they'd met. All those times when things had felt familiar between them. Why she'd asked him out to dinner even though he worked for her. Why she trusted him when she hadn't trusted anyone outside of her family in years.

There was something inside her that did remember him. And even if that hadn't been true, she felt something for him now. She loved him. These last weeks had been enough for her to know that. So even if something she couldn't remember had created that pull, she'd acted on it. *She* had. And she had done so *now*. And that was significant, wasn't it?

If only all of it didn't feel so wrapped up in emotion that wouldn't allow her to accept it.

She blinked, realising she'd been lost in thought. But he didn't seem to mind. He was still staring at her.

'Surely this dress isn't that gobsmacking?' she commented dryly.

'It's pretty damn gobsmacking.' He tilted his head, lifting his eyes to hers. 'Is that how one should use that word?'

'If "one" refers to me, then, yes, because that's how I just used the word.'

His lips twitched before that sombre expression took over again. 'You're clearly on your way somewhere...' He trailed off in a way that made it clear he wanted to know where.

'The app launch.'

'That's tonight?' He was rolling his eyes before he finished. 'Of course it's tonight. Tia's contract to work for you ended today.'

A punch landed in her gut. She steeled herself

so it wouldn't cause her to stagger back. She'd forgotten that today was the last day of her contract with the housekeeping agency. She'd forgotten that today would be the last day he'd be working for her.

It was silly to feel disappointed since for pretty much half of the time, she hadn't seen him. But she'd known he was there. She'd known he was cooking for her and cleaning for her.

She would have been ashamed of taking pleasure in that knowledge, but it wasn't because she was on some kind of power trip. She just felt more secure with him doing those things for her. It was a form of caring she was no longer used to, even if she was paying for it.

She wasn't sure if that made her pathetic or not.

'Why are you here?' she asked softly.

He swallowed. 'I'll come back.'

'No, Tyler,' she said, before he could turn away. 'Just…say it.'

He stared at her for a long time. She wished she knew whether that meant he would answer her. Whether he would tell her the reason he'd shown up at her door now, on the final day of his contract.

Just when she thought he might, Dom called out from the lounge.

'Everything okay, B?'

She looked over her shoulder, saw him walking towards her. 'Yes,' she said primly.

She turned to Tyler. His expression had gone from sombre to unreadable. She tilted her head. Wondered at the reason for it. Then she realised how it looked. Dom in his tux, her in a dress, the night of the launch.

'Tyler, this is Dom,' she said, shifting so that Dom could stand next to her. 'My brother.'

Tyler's eyes flitted to hers. Relief mixed with something else, something she couldn't quite identify, but looked fierce and passionate, rested there.

Seconds later, before she could even try to name it, Tyler shook it off and held out a hand. 'Nice to meet you, Dom.'

Dom studied the hand, but didn't wait too long before he took it. 'Tyler,' he acknowledged. 'The housekeeper, right?' He paused. 'And also the man my sister is seeing.'

'Dom,' she warned.

Tyler merely gave Dom a steady look. 'I'm not sure either one of us would classify it that way, but a version of that is certainly true.'

'It is?' she asked, surprise more than anything taking control of her tongue. 'I mean, it is,' she confirmed, nodding to Dom.

Dom gave her the look he saved for when she was being stupid. She couldn't even call him out on it. She had just done something stupid. She'd doubted the qualification the man she loved tried to provide for their relationship out loud, and then she'd tried to cover it up.

She was a mess.

'You should be the one going with her this evening,' said Dom.

Her attention snapped to her brother. 'No,' she said, in another warning. 'Don't get involved.'

'You want him with you, Brooke,' Dom said casually, as if she'd already offered the information to the world and he wasn't sharing a secret she didn't want anyone to know—let alone her brother and the object of what could only be described as an obsession. 'You should take him.'

'Dom, can I speak to you privately for a moment?' she asked through her teeth. 'Tyler, you can wait inside.'

Without waiting to see how he responded to her command, she grabbed her brother's arm and marched him to the kitchen.

'What are you doing?' she snapped. 'You need to have my back, not make things more complicated.'

'Am I wrong?'

'You—' She cut herself off before she admitted something she wasn't ready to admit. 'It doesn't matter.'

'Except it does, B,' he said, stepping closer and brushing a hand over her hair. Her styled hair.

She swatted at his hand. He ignored her.

'I was wondering why you were acting so strange, but when he showed up it made sense. And then you introduced him to me, not the other way around. You were more concerned about him thinking we were a couple than you were about my opinion. That means something.'

'I don't…'

'You don't have to.'

Dom's words were gentle and he was right, despite the fact that she hadn't even finished her sentence.

'I keep telling you this. You don't have to have all the answers right at the beginning. It's okay to work your way through it.'

It seemed pointless now to tell Dom that she did have to have the answers. She couldn't risk everything she would risk for the *chance* of something.

'I don't think I can ask him to go with me,' she said honestly, because it was the only answer she could give. 'It's short notice, and he doesn't have a tux, and—'

Dom was walking out before she could stop him.

'You and I are about the same size, aren't we?' Dom asked Tyler.

'Dom—'

'I think so,' Tyler replied, interrupting what would have been her protest.

'Cool. Do you want to wear this so you can go with my sister tonight?' Dom didn't wait for an answer. 'We can change in the spare bedroom.'

'Brooke,' Tyler said. 'Do you want me to go with you?'

Dom grunted. It was in approval, she knew, because she had long since learnt the nuances of his grunts.

Tyler looked faintly alarmed, but his eyes were still on her, as if her answer was more important than her brother's faintly threatening sounds.

'Do you want to go with me?' she asked.

Dom's snort made her glare at him. But then Tyler answered, and she forgot Dom was even in the room.

'Very much so.'

Her lips parted and she nodded, hoping he'd understand that she was saying she did, indeed, want him with her. And it seemed he did. He gestured to Dom, who thankfully didn't comment, and they were both gone a second later.

She paced the room, trying not to worry about the fact that her brother was alone with Tyler. Or vice versa, for that matter. She hadn't told Dom about her and Tyler's past together. Wouldn't tell him—she was too ashamed.

But should she really be ashamed of what she couldn't remember? *Yes*, her brain answered for her. Because not remembering it didn't change the fact that she had done it.

She hadn't ever particularly cared that she suffered from amnesia. She didn't want to remember what had been the most traumatic time in her life. What she *could* remember wasn't easy or pleasant, so she had never begrudged her mind for trying to protect itself and her.

Now, though... She wished she could remember what it had been like. What had been going through her mind? What had she felt during those dinners together? Had she made Tyler believe she wanted him to kiss her? Had she initiated the kiss?

She didn't have answers to many of those questions, but there were some Tyler could offer her. And she didn't think it was wrong of her to want them. She simply hadn't asked for them before because that would have entailed talking to Tyler, which would have required seeing him.

But she was seeing him now. She could ask those questions and maybe get some closure. Except that implied the conclusion of whatever was happening between her and Tyler, and that felt oddly painful.

Even though she didn't know what to do about her feelings for him.

Even though she knew he might be leaving.

Even though their past and their future seemed so misaligned.

The doorbell rang, and this time she knew it was the car. She told the driver they'd be there in a second, got all her things ready, then waited for Tyler at the door.

She caught her breath a little when he came out of the spare bedroom. The tux fitted him perfectly, though it looked entirely different on him than it had on Dom.

Perhaps because she didn't feel as if the air around Dom was electric. Magnetic, with an answering magnet inside her, demanding that she go to Tyler. Curl herself around him or against him, she wasn't fussy.

She took a breath to steady herself. 'You look nice.'

'Thanks,' he said.

'Funny, you didn't tell me that when I wore it,' said her brother.

'It would have been weird if I had,' she told Dom with a shrewd look. 'Are you ready to go?' she asked Tyler.

'If you are.'

They walked to the car.

Brooke tried to ignore the wave Dom gave them as they drove off. But he was doing it so damn happily, as if he were proud of himself for setting this up.

'Why do I feel like a kid being waved off to prom?' Tyler asked.

Brooke snorted. 'That's exactly what I was thinking. Well, not exactly. Also I doubt he would ever wave off his own kid that happily.

Dom's more the scowling parent type, if that makes sense.'

'Since I used to have one, it does.'

'Your mom?'

'Dad.'

He curled his fingers, but Brooke didn't think he noticed.

'He wasn't the approving kind. Not initially, anyway. And his disapproval was more directed towards Tia than me.'

'So he was a misogynist?' she said, trying to lighten the mood. Although, in hindsight, insulting his father probably wasn't the way to do it.

But Tyler agreed easily. 'Pretty much. Although I guess I can understand it. She was always more vulnerable than me.'

'Because she was a girl?'

'Because she's Tia.' He paused. 'I know you haven't met her, but she's fierce. Except it's all mostly on the outside, for the sake of the world. Deep down, she's…sensitive.'

Something about the way he said it made Brooke search his expression. Pain tightened the skin around his eyes, his mouth. She wasn't sure how she knew that it was pain, but she did.

'You told her about London,' she guessed.

His head whipped towards her. 'How did you know?'

'I'm not sure,' she answered honestly. 'A gut feeling?'

His eyes softened. Something softened inside her as well. She was certain that something was her heart, but acknowledging it felt as though she was approving of it when really, she desperately wanted her heart to behave. Things were too uncertain for it not to.

'How did she take it?' she asked, trying to distract herself and her organs.

He exhaled. 'About as well as you would expect.'

'Ah… So she didn't care that you're considering leaving, only that you waited so long to talk to her about it because you believed she wouldn't support you. Because you were using her as an excuse to avoid facing the real issue, which is your feelings about yourself and your father.'

He stared at her. 'Is this your gut again?'

She shrugged. 'I've made some deductions during our time together.'

'No kidding.' He shook his head. 'I guess I could have handled this entire thing better.'

'We all usually think that, looking back.'

'It's strange, isn't it? We can psych ourselves up about something. Make it worse than it is when in reality, it's simple.'

She angled a look at him. 'Why do I feel as though you're not only talking about your sister?'

'I'm not sure,' he said easily, though the expression on his face told her she was right.

When he shifted the conversation back to his sister, it seemed to prove that he was deflecting.

'Tia did care that I wanted to leave. Not as much as I thought she would—I blame my ego for that—but in a normal way. A healthy way,' he added, almost as an afterthought.

'In the same way you care that you're thinking of leaving?' she asked. 'Because you'll miss her and your nephew.'

'Yes.' He paused. 'As for the other stuff… We didn't get to that. *I* didn't get to that.' Another pause. 'But you're right. This is about my dad, and my not wanting to be like him.'

The sadness in his voice had her reaching for his hand. 'You're not like him, Tyler. Deep down, you know that. And not only because I've told you so a million times. You know it deep in your gut.' Her hand tightened. 'You're scared, and that's okay. It's okay to be scared. But you have control of this. *You* do—not your father.'

She waited to see if he would respond. When he didn't, she pushed on, needing him to believe her.

'You chose to tell your sister and get her opinion on the situation. She might need some time, but she wants you to be happy so she'll choose to support you. Once you're in London, you can manage your time. You can keep in touch with your family. Arrange visits for Tia and Nyle.

And you can come back,' she pointed out softly. 'Whenever you like. To visit, to keep in touch. You can make Cape Town your base again once you've set everything up. All of that is in your control, Tyler. Don't allow anything to make you think otherwise.'

He didn't reply for a long time, and she watched him. It felt as though she was watching the sun rise over the darkest hills. The shadows on his face faded, his shoulders loosened. She swore she could see the muscles in the rest of his body ease, too. And when he looked at her, his face brighter than she'd seen in a long time, she felt that sun shining on her. Warming the coldest parts inside her, shining light on the feelings she'd shoved into the crevices of her heart, her mind.

She loved this man, who cared so deeply for his family. Who took his responsibilities seriously. Who didn't push her for answers she didn't have or ask her for things she couldn't give.

A deep, crushing sadness moved over the light, even though she desperately tried to clutch it in her hands. Desperately tried to keep the darkness from creeping into her soul. What was the point of sadness when she couldn't pinpoint the root of it? When she couldn't express why she felt the way she did? When she only knew the sadness was different from the precious feelings she had for Tyler?

'You've simplified things I've been complicating for a long time,' he commented.

His words felt as warm as the hand still in hers. 'Only if it works.'

'I... I need time to think it through. But I think... I think I can see that there's no danger of me becoming like my father when we're different people. Our priorities are different.' He ran his tongue over his teeth. 'I want to know that Tia's on board with any decision I make. I want us to make it as a family. There never was that with him. He decided and we had to accept that. I think that's what hurt my mom the most.'

'And he doesn't even know what he lost because of that decision,' she said. 'That's his punishment. A life without knowing who you and Tia have become. A life without knowing his grandchild. It was in his control to make decisions that would have changed that, but he didn't.' She shook her head. 'There's no danger of you becoming like him at all, Tyler. At the very core of it, you're too good a man to allow that.'

'You're too good a man to allow that.'
The words carved themselves into his mind the moment she said them. Not because he believed them, but because she'd said them.

Brooke thought he was a good man. And even if that wasn't true—though he'd like to believe it was—the very fact that she thought it made him want to be a good man. He would do anything and everything he could to become the man she thought he was.

It helped, of course, that she had pointed out his power in the situation. He had been so focused on his issues with his father that he hadn't recognised that power. But now he could see the possibilities. The *choices*. This didn't have to be permanent. This didn't have to take him away from his family. He would talk to Tia and Nyle as often as he could. He'd visit them, or they'd visit him. This opportunity wouldn't mean the end of their family.

If only he had come to that conclusion before hurting his sister.

She was disappointed that he hadn't trusted her, she'd said.

'Didn't you think I'd want this for you? Did you really believe I would keep you from doing something that excites you because of my fears?'

But she was still afraid—he had seen it. He couldn't blame her when that was the curse of what their father had done to them. Only Tia didn't shy away from making tough decisions because of it, like he had. She faced them. Even if she had said she needed some time before she could talk to him without wanting to kick him for being so stupid.

Despite that, he was cautiously hopeful for the future. Until he thought about Brooke, about where his leaving would leave *them*.

He hadn't known what to expect when he'd shown up at her door. Did he want to tell her he loved her? Tell her about what had happened with Tia? Ask her how she was feeling about everything?

It was likely a combination of all three. There was an urgency to it, too, since after today there would be no more chances to 'accidentally' bump into her. There would only be intentional meetings from here on out. Which was why he was here, accompanying her at the launch party.

She looked beautiful. Her green dress was loose, but skilfully arranged over her body, showing peeks of her breasts at its neckline, of her right leg through the slit. She blended in with her surroundings here at the venue, where green vines draped around wooden arches and high, steady mountains rose all around them.

They'd driven quite a distance to get there, but Brooke's company had once been situated close by, and it was still their tradition to hold launch events here.

He could see the appeal. They'd driven up a winding road to get to the top of a hill, and the restaurant overlooked the Stellenbosch area, giving magnificent views of the mountains surrounding them. It was secluded and private, felt expensive and high class, and he understood now why he'd had to wear the tuxedo.

Although merely standing next to Brooke demanded that he be dressed equally formally. He wanted to say equally stunningly, but he didn't think that was possible.

Her hair had been swept back, much as it had been that night at his business event, but this time, it was parted in the middle. Somehow it gave greater prominence to her face. It seemed sharper, more distinct this evening. He didn't know if that was because she'd put on make-up or because his mind was marking every single feature.

This night felt significant, though it was too early to tell why.

He exhaled.

'I thought I was the one who was meant to be nervous,' Brooke said mildly at his side.

'I'm not nervous,' he said automatically.

She merely lifted an eyebrow. He felt as if someone had thrown a piece of him into hot oil.

No, an inner voice told him. *You cannot muddle things with desire now.*

'*Are* you nervous?' he asked, shifting direction. 'You don't seem like it.'

'She's never nervous,' one of Brooke's coworkers said, stopping in front of them. It was an older woman he'd been introduced to earlier—

as Brooke's 'friend'—but he couldn't recall her name now.

'Nonsense, Sharon,' Brooke said, waving the words off.

She winked at him. It took him a second to realise she'd used the woman's name for his sake. He offered her a grateful smile.

'I am nervous,' she continued, directing her answer to Sharon. 'I just try not to show it. My team doesn't need their manager pacing about.'

'See what I mean?' Sharon said with a smile. 'This is pretty much how she is at every launch of hers.'

'This is only the third.'

'In five years. That's more than many others in your position.'

'Sharon,' Brooke said, waving a hand. A blush reddened her cheeks. 'Stop!'

'And that's another winning characteristic: humility. If she weren't so damn efficient, I'd probably fire her for it.'

Sharon smiled and left them alone.

Both he and Brooke stared after her for a moment, then Tyler turned to her. 'That's your boss?'

'Yeah.' She frowned. 'I'm pretty sure I told you that.'

'That's not the point. The point is that she clearly thinks you're amazing. You shouldn't be humble. You should be basking in her praise.'

The colour flooding Brooke's face was like a flower blooming on a spring day. Innocent, pure, beautiful. His lips were curving before he could stop them.

'What?' Brooke asked defensively. 'Why are you smiling at me like that?'

'You're cute when you're embarrassed.'

'I am not embarrassed.' But the red deepened.

He was full-out grinning now. 'Why are you embarrassed by praise?'

'I'm just doing my job, Tyler.'

'Sounds like you're doing it pretty damn well.'

'Isn't that how you're meant to work?' she demanded. 'You're not supposed to be mediocre. I know you don't believe that, so why are you making me feel bad?'

'Am I? I thought I was giving you a compliment.'

'I…well…okay.' She took a breath. 'Thank you.'

He bit his lip to keep himself from smiling again. People were looking at them, and he didn't want them to think he was deranged. He knew it was curiosity, and he'd bet anything that Brooke didn't usually bring people to her launch parties.

Besides family, he corrected, thinking about Dom. And about what Dom told him when they'd been changing.

The fact that she wants you with her tonight means something. Don't mess that up.

A warning and a revelation in one. And that was why he wasn't going to talk to her about anything other than the launch.

'I'm glad you asked me to come tonight,' he said softly. Because he couldn't resist it, he reached out and ran the hair falling over her shoulder between his fingers. 'I get to see you in a different light.'

'Do you…?' She stopped and looked away from him, but seconds later looked back.

Determination glinted in her eyes. Damn if that didn't make him love her more.

'Do you like what you get to see?'

'How could I not?'

She smiled, the determination eclipsed by a warmth he was sure he didn't deserve.

The moment didn't last—someone wanted her attention for something—but it stayed with him the entire night.

A night he spent watching her watching those around her.

He'd never felt more content in his life.

CHAPTER FIFTEEN

SHE COULDN'T DESCRIBE how relieved she was that everything had gone smoothly. She might have been acting cool in front of everyone—it hadn't been humility as much as a display of confidence for her team's sake—but she'd been worried. This might be her third project, but it had been the most challenging. It had required all her skill and ingenuity, and that of her team, and she'd been holding her breath pretty much the entire time.

That might have been because of Tyler, too, but she wasn't ready to think about that. As it was, she was already having a hard time with him in the car.

The drive was almost an hour long, and forty minutes had gone by with them chatting idly about the evening. Now they were quiet, which allowed her to focus on other things. Like how, despite the fact that he was wearing her brother's tux, Tyler smelled like himself. A heady, tempting smell that made her want to curl into his side and sniff him.

Sniff him? Good heavens, she was losing her mind.

'When we get back do you want to share some celebratory champagne?' she asked, turning to him and surprising herself.

He looked over, smiled a gentle smile, and said, 'I'd love to.'

How did that turn her to mush?

At least it kept her distracted until they got home.

He waited in the garden while she got the champagne and glasses, but immediately got up to help her as soon as she returned.

'To you,' he said, when he'd poured them each a glass.

'To the team who made it possible.'

'Still not able to take a compliment, huh?' he teased, but he clinked his glass against hers and took a sip.

She didn't answer, drank from her own glass, and enjoyed the way the bubbles felt over her tongue. Then she sighed and kicked off her shoes, putting her feet up on the chair in front of her.

'It's been a long eighteen months,' she said with a sigh.

'You've been working on that project for eighteen months?'

'Yeah. Some days it feels like it was for ever. Some days it feels like it was just a few weeks.'

She shook her head. 'I'm glad it's over. We have to monitor for bugs and do updates, of course, but the app itself is out there and I'm relieved.' She looked over at him. 'I imagine this is how you're going to feel once you get things established in London.'

With that, the air between them changed. She hadn't meant it to, but something about the way Tyler held himself made her realise it had. She tried to think about what she'd said, but it had only been an allusion to him leaving. Why would that upset him? There had been no judgement in her tone. She'd been trying to be supportive, for heaven's sake, even though his leaving would break her heart.

Besides, they'd spoken about it before, in the car. He hadn't seemed upset about the situation when they'd been talking about Tia. Which made Brooke think that this was about *her*, which hardly seemed fair.

'I've always wanted to ask why you have such an incredible garden,' he said.

The words came out of nowhere, and Brooke had to take time to readjust. Tension crept over her. Irrationally, she wondered if that had been his intention all along. Had he known she'd done it for Kian and wanted to give her something to be upset about?

But that wasn't possible. He didn't know about

Kian. Unless she'd told him during their time together and she couldn't remember it. He'd said they'd never talked about anything personal. He hadn't known she was married. So maybe not?

'My husband was a landscape designer. We met at college and dated for a while before we got married. When we did, we were too poor to have our dream house. So he drew up this plan for our for ever home one day. I... I didn't ever tell you?' she asked, to be sure. 'About my husband, I mean? When we were...during that week?'

She saw the confusion in his eyes under the garden lights around them—one of which he'd replaced—but it quickly cleared, replaced by understanding.

'No. I didn't know you were married. I didn't know about your husband.'

'Okay.'

'You did nothing wrong,' he added softly, and the words were almost carried away with the night breeze. 'That week...it was friendship, Brooke. We were friends.'

'Except we kissed,' she scoffed. 'And we didn't talk about anything personal. How could that be "friendship"?'

He set his glass down, shifted so his elbows rested on his knees. 'We talked about important things. Things we valued. You knew I cared about my family. I knew you cared about yours, too.' He paused. 'It was clear that something had hurt you, and you were steering clear of that. So I didn't push, and you didn't push me.' He took a breath. 'I was dealing with some stuff back then, too. My nephew was just born and my mother wasn't there to see it. Neither was my father, for that matter.'

There was a lingering silence, but he continued.

'We were friends, Brooke. The kiss was a...a mistake.' He looked at her. 'When we were together it was like the world didn't exist. The world and our responsibilities. That night, it got to us. We had too much wine and the chemistry that had made us get along so well turned into something more. But it stopped before it started and we both... We both knew it was a mistake.'

Something about the way he'd said it made her wonder. 'Did we?' she asked. 'Did *we* both know that?'

He took a moment to reply, but when he did, his voice was steady. 'What do you want me to say, Brooke? That I knew it was a mistake because you pushed me away almost as soon as our lips touched? That you looked distraught and I knew that even though we were both a little tipsy we shouldn't have done it?'

She opened her mouth, but couldn't reply. Not with what she wanted to say, which was that she was relieved she'd responded that way. That she was relieved they'd been drinking and hadn't been thinking like themselves.

She didn't think she had to say it though. Tyler was studying her too intently, seeing too much. He knew her, knew versions of her that even she couldn't remember. She had no doubt he knew what she was thinking.

'If you want to know more about that time, Brooke, you only have to ask,' he offered. 'I'll tell you everything you need to know.'

'Thank you.'

She wished she didn't have to ask any of the questions she had, but they spilled over her lips anyway.

What had she told him? How had she been? Had he thought it strange they weren't talking about their lives? What had he told her? And were things different now? How?

He answered each question thoroughly, patiently. And each answer did make it seem as if they had been friends. Until those last two questions, at which he paused. Looked at her.

'I think you know the answer to those two questions.'

'Do I?' she asked lightly.

He turned the watch at his wrist. The action was so deliberate that she shifted. Curled her feet under her. Folded her arms.

'Yes, things are different,' he answered. 'I know more about you now than I ever did then. I understand how complicated this is for you.'

'It's complicated for you, too.'

'And that's different, too. It was easy then. We only saw one another for a few hours a day. We met up, ate things we liked, then left and didn't know anything about where the other person was. I had to trust that you were safe. That you had people around you who would keep you safe.'

'And now?'

'Now...' He took a deep breath. 'Now I need to be sure you're safe. I want to be one of the people who keeps you that way.'

She stared. 'Tyler—'

'I know it's complicated,' he said over her interruption. 'I know none of this is fair, and that having this conversation is only going to complicate things even more. But you asked how things are different, and the answer is this. Back then, I was enamoured, sure. I thought you were beautiful, compassionate and smart. But I was okay with being your friend.'

She almost didn't want to ask, but she did it anyway. 'Now you're not?'

He shook his head. 'Now I'm in love with you, Brooke. Your beauty comes from how you look, of course, but it's *because* you're compassionate and you're smart. You work hard, you love hard.

And you constantly want to do more. Now I can't be your friend.' He met her eyes. 'And you don't want to be mine either.'

Her fists clutched at the material of her dress, but because her arms were folded she didn't think Tyler could see it.

In her mind, she was completely fine with him seeing her as cool and aloof, as if she were taking this information steadily and it didn't cause her heart to beat harder than it had in years. In reality, she was tense. She knew Tyler would soon look at her and see someone who was panicking.

And yet he remained steady. He looked at her with the kind of confidence he shouldn't have after declaring his love for her. Unless he was that sure she felt the same way.

'What does it matter?' she asked, not even caring that her question revealed that she did feel the same way. 'I have baggage heavier than I can carry sometimes. And you...you're leaving.'

'But you love me?'

She exhaled, impatient with the question when he already had the answer. 'Yes, Tyler. But what does it matter?'

'What do you mean, what does it matter? It *does* matter,' he insisted. 'If we feel the same way about one another, surely we can work out the rest?'

'How do we work out that I feel guilty about

falling for you?' Words spilled out of her mouth now, no filter—which she would no doubt regret. 'I mean, I had been working it out until I realised that I was probably falling for you the week after my husband died. I was working out my grief by starting a "friendship" with you—' she used air quotes '—and how can I make that okay?'

He blinked. Then blinked again as he leaned back in his chair. His expression was unreadable, with none of the passion he'd been speaking with earlier shadowing his face.

'That's how you feel?' he asked.

'Isn't that what happened?' she replied, even though it didn't feel right. None of this did. 'How do I reconcile what I feel for you now with what happened back then?'

'No,' he replied woodenly, 'what you really want to know is how you can reconcile what you feel for me now with what you feel for your husband.'

'No. *No.* I'm ready to move on. Just…not with you.' She closed her eyes. 'I didn't mean it like that. I meant not with what's happened between us.'

'Okay,' he said, straightening. 'If that's what you need to believe.'

'What I need to—?' She broke off, standing now, too. 'Tyler, you're leaving. You're *leaving*.'

'So come with me.'

Her mouth fell open. She shut it quickly, afraid that her heart was beating so voraciously it would jump out given the chance.

When she was finally able to speak again, she didn't recognise her voice. 'I should come with you? Leave my family, my job—everything I've worked for in the last five years?'

'We'll figure it out.'

He seemed unaware of the desperate edge to his tone.

'And what happens when you're done in London, Tyler?' she asked. 'When you want to come back? Do I leave whatever I've built there *again*?' She shook her head before he could answer. 'I built a life around a man before and it didn't work out because of something entirely outside our control. I can't... I can't let go of the stability I've worked so hard for since then. I... I...can't.'

'Even for the sake of us?'

'Are you listening to yourself? Are you listening to *me*?'

He looked as if he were about to answer, but no words came from his mouth. Slowly, she saw him realise what he'd asked, what was happening. He took a step back, then another. Took a deep breath, then another.

'I... I'm sorry. I didn't...' His eyes met hers, the plea in them clear. 'I didn't realise...'

She didn't have anything to say to that. There

was too much panic in her brain, in her body, for her to be receptive to an apology. To an explanation.

'I love you,' he said, a long time later.

'And I love you,' she replied. 'But that doesn't change anything.'

She was faintly aware that she was pushing him away. That she was closing herself down to protect herself in any way she could. But when she succeeded and he left, she didn't feel protected at all. She only felt empty.

And, standing in the garden her deceased husband had designed for them, she also felt alone.

CHAPTER SIXTEEN

'YOU'RE STILL MOPING AROUND? It's been three months since you stopped working for Brooke!' Tia said, eyeing Tyler.

Two months, two weeks, four days, to be exact.

Tyler didn't respond with that, though. Instead he glowered at her, before turning his attention to his nephew. Nyle was fascinated by the trains at King's Cross Station, his eyes going wide each time one stopped. Too fascinated to pay attention to the adults in his family.

'He's not going to help you,' Tia commented. 'He's been like this since we got on the train at the airport.'

'Has it only been a month since I left?' he asked blandly. 'I have missed you so.'

She stuck out her tongue and he smiled because, damn it, he *had* missed her. She'd called him a week after he'd finally told her about the expansion opportunity because she was ready to talk. When they had, of course she'd supported him. She'd needed some time to get her head around it, she'd said, but she wanted the best for him.

The remaining weeks he'd spent negotiating his contract with his new business partners, convincing Tia to look after June while he was gone, and then preparing to live in London.

He'd wanted that preparation to include closure with Brooke, but he hadn't known how that could happen. He'd messed up royally, and he had no idea how to fix things.

The realisation had haunted him before and after he'd left. She hadn't contacted him; he hadn't contacted her. The best thing for both of them to do was to accept things were over.

Except he hadn't been able to do that in the last five years—when he hadn't even been in love with her. It sure as hell wasn't going to be easy now that he was. Especially when he knew he had pushed her too hard, too fast. He *knew* it. He had panicked, had thought being together was better than being apart, and he hadn't realised how much it would scare her.

When he had realised, it had been too late. He'd realised he was forcing her to make a decision she didn't want to make for *his* sake. His fear had pushed him into his father's territory. He had stopped before he'd put a flag into the land and declared it his own, but he was horrified. And so was she.

So, yeah, he had no idea how to fix that.

'Are you going to keep moping, or can we get going?' asked Tia.

Tyler didn't bother answering, but he made a concerted effort to let go of his melancholy. It was his constant companion. When he was lucky he could forget it, but those moments never lasted for long. Not when he wanted to talk to Brooke about the opportunity of his lifetime. Not when he saw the vibrancy of London, noticed its moods, enjoyed its people and wanted to share it with her.

But for his sister and nephew he would try harder.

He thought he was doing well until his sister heaved a sigh during dinner and said, 'Maybe you should come back home.'

'What?'

'Come home and fix things with Brooke.' She helped Nyle with his food, the restaurant's signature pizza. 'You're clearly not going to be happy until you do, and what's the point of even being here if you're not happy?'

'I *am* happy,' he said stubbornly. 'Besides, you don't know what happened between me and Brooke.'

'I know enough.'

'How?'

'You're not together.'

It was a simple answer he had no comeback for.

'Plus, she's miserable, too, so clearly whatever happened isn't what either of you—'

'Wait—what? How do you know that?'

'Oh, didn't I tell you?' she said smugly. 'Brooke called the agency with a glowing recommendation of my work and asked if I could work for her permanently.'

He stared at her. The only thing that came to his mind was, 'I thought they only dealt with temporary jobs?'

'They do, which is why they said no. But then she called me directly, made me an offer I couldn't refuse, and now we're here.' She stole an olive off Nyle's pizza and popped it into her mouth.

'And you're only telling me this now?' he asked slowly. 'How long have you been working for her?'

'A couple of weeks.'

'Again—you're only telling me this *now*?'

'I thought it would have more impact if I told you in person.' Her eyes sparkled at him.

'There's a lot about this that bothers me...'

'And we'll get to all of it, I'm sure.'

'But the foremost question I have right now is *why*?' he continued, as if she hadn't interrupted him.

'It's a good opportunity. And it comes with

insane benefits, like the fact that she's letting me bring Nyle to her house after school and will give me as many sick days as I need. Also, she's told me that June can come over to play with Mochi whenever I want. I almost asked her to look after June while we were over here, but I thought that might be too awkward. We left June with a friend.'

He closed his eyes, letting the information run through his brain. 'You've had good opportunities before,' he said slowly, and opened his eyes. 'And if I'd known you wanted something like this I would have—'

'No,' she interrupted. 'I didn't want to work for my brother. Nor for any of his rich acquaintances who see the help as being beneath them.'

'You don't even *know* Brooke!' he exclaimed. 'How do you know she's not like them?'

'Because you wouldn't have fallen in love with her if she was.'

He hadn't told her that, but of course she knew. He sighed in answer, hoping the tension would rush out of him like air from a balloon. But no. He was still curling his fingers under the table, his shoulders still felt as if there were boulders on them, and he was still actively trying not to frown, so as not to upset his nephew.

'I also would have quit if she was terrible,' Tia

continued, oblivious to his turmoil—or perhaps not caring.

'And you would have lost your job with the agency in the process.'

'I would have found another. And this way, I can spy for you.'

He resisted for all of ten seconds. 'In what way?'

'I've already told you she's miserable.'

'That's it?'

'What more do you want?'

'I don't know,' he answered because he really didn't know what he wanted. It was unlikely that Brooke would tell Tia if she wanted to be with him.

Huh. Maybe he *did* know what he wanted.

'Do you want to tell me what happened?' Tia asked.

'Not really.'

He told her anyway, since she already knew everything that had happened except for the argument that last night.

To her credit, she didn't say anything. Not even when he told her about his stupid request for Brooke to come to London with him. She just listened in between eating and helping Nyle to eat, nodding in encouragement or acknowledgement every now and then.

When he was done, she said, 'I feel partially responsible.'

'Why?' he asked. 'Because you made me hope things would work out when you told me that love would conquer all?'

'I did *not* say that.'

He gave her a look.

'Okay, fine, I said something like that. But I hoped…' She heaved out a sigh. 'I think I made you think you needed to figure it out right at that minute, when really you both needed time. She probably needed more time than you.'

'Yes, I can see that now,' he said dryly.

'So why are you still here?'

'What do you mean?'

'Well, if you're still miserable, I figure you didn't tell her that. She doesn't know that you regret pushing her and that you'll give her as much space as she needs. That you'll be there when she's ready, whenever that might be. Assuming you will be, of course,' she added.

His initial answer was yes . He had spent five years waiting—what was five more? Ten more? But he knew he had to give himself time to think it through.

He gave himself until the night before Tia and Nyle were due to leave, actually. He sat up after they'd gone to bed, trying to think about what it would mean to commit to Brooke in that way.

No matter what angle he came to it from, he reached the same conclusion. He loved her. He wanted to spend his life with her. And, after what he'd said to her that night, he needed to prove that he was serious about it.

So he booked himself on the same flight back to South Africa as his family.

When Tia found him the next morning, she took one look at his face and said, 'Don't get me fired.'

'I can't promise that,' he replied, hope curving his lips into a grin.

It made him feel lighter than he had in a long time. Which turned out to be a good thing, since that feeling of weightlessness helped him duck when Tia threw a pillow at him.

Brooke didn't spend her days missing Tyler. No, sir. She spent them working. Fixing bugs or anticipating them. Helping with other projects. Since she had come out of the first phase of her project, and the second phase required time to figure out how Phase One would affect it, she had free time, too. She spent it wisely. When she got home, she put everything into training Mochi, which was bittersweet.

Every time she succeeded she would hear Tyler's voice in her head telling her she was doing a good job. Every time she failed she'd hear him saying it was because she wasn't being assertive enough. Or she would hear him tell her to keep trying, which she did. Not because he was telling her—even though it was only a mental version of him—but because she knew Mochi needed consistency. That was what the training videos she watched and the books she read said. And, to their credit, it was working.

Mochi seemed happier than he had been in months. He was thriving. He loved having a friend to play with whenever June came to visit. Which was bittersweet as well because it never failed to remind her of Tyler.

Dom had attributed Mochi's behaviour to the fact that Brooke was at home more, that dogs loved having their humans close by. He was probably right. Hell, she thought he might have been right about Mochi all along. The dog seemed quite fond of her now. And she thought that she might have been pushing Mochi away, too, thinking that he didn't like her.

Which made her wonder how much she had sabotaged things with Tyler. Clearly, if she couldn't accept love from a dog, she wouldn't be able to accept it from a human.

It took her a long time to figure out she was scared. Scared of being robbed of that love again. She made an appointment with her therapist to talk it through. It helped, even if he did tell her things she'd already known he would say.

Her biggest takeaway was the fact that it was okay that she needed time. Except it didn't *feel* okay. Not when Tyler hadn't been able to give it to her and she felt as if she'd robbed them both of something beautiful.

Over time though, she stopped blaming herself so much and started blaming him a little more. Why hadn't he realised that she needed time? That everything was happening too fast and the information about their past would make it seem even more like lightning speed? Why hadn't he thought about how losing her husband would affect her ability to be in a relationship?

Because you didn't say any of that to him.

It was an annoying realisation to have when, again, she absolutely did *not* spend time thinking about him.

Mochi started barking, giving her a reason to stop thinking about what she wasn't thinking about.

'Oh, you're hearing Tia, are you?' she asked him, though he'd already sprinted through the trees for the back door.

She could leave it open these days since Mochi spent any time she was in the garden at her side.

It was more comforting than she'd anticipated, the dog's company. As was Tia's. She only saw her new housekeeper in the mornings, and sometimes after work if she came home early. When she did, she got to see Nyle, too. And seeing Tyler's family made her feel as though he wasn't so far away even as it reminded her of his absence.

Sometimes, when she walked into the house and heard people in it, she still thought it was Tyler. And Tia and Nyle's faces held enough of Tyler's features that her heart would stall when she saw them—and then break when she realised they weren't him.

Still, she wouldn't trade it for anything. Not when they were her only connection to him.

She could hardly believe it had been three months. She had felt this emptiness echo inside her for *three months*.

And she'd believed she'd succeeded in not thinking about him. She was a fool.

With an exhalation, she walked back to the house. Her lighter workload meant she didn't have to work the same hours she had during the last project, but she did have to show her face at the office at a reasonable time.

She stopped when she saw Tyler crouched on the patio, rubbing Mochi's belly.

Until the moment he lifted his head and met her eyes, Brooke was pretty sure he was an apparition. Seeing him was just one small step away from hearing his voice, after all. But she wouldn't have been able to conjure up that little jolt of electricity she felt when their gazes locked. Or the way her stomach felt as if it were an eagle, swooping down from the sky.

No, an apparition wouldn't have had that effect.

'Hey,' he said, his voice both familiar and unfamiliar.

She wanted to record it, play it back when this was over, so she never had to feel as if it was unfamiliar again. Only she wasn't sure she wanted her skin to feel so aware at the sound of it every time.

'Hi,' she said.

'You probably want to know what I'm doing here?'

She tilted her head. 'It's definitely one of my questions,' she allowed. 'The others are: what are you doing in South Africa and how did you get into my house?'

'Tia let me in.' He straightened. 'She's aware that it's a violation, but she's trusting that I won't screw this up again and it won't matter.'

Her breath caught, but he didn't notice. Instead, he looked up at the house.

'I think she's somewhere upstairs now, trying to give us privacy while desperately wanting to know what's happening and figuring out if she still has a job.'

Brooke took a second. 'Well, I'm not thrilled she's letting people into my house, but I'll let her off with a warning. I didn't hire her so I could fire her. Even if she has given me this really good reason to.'

'I don't think she thought I was "people,"' he said, with a wry twist of his mouth.

It didn't hide the hurt in his eyes.

She wished she could be immune to it. He had hurt her, too. More than she'd thought possible. Her therapist had told her it was a good sign. That if she hurt more than she'd thought possible, she probably cared more than she'd thought possible, too.

Surprisingly, that didn't make her feel better.

'Can I ask you a question?' he asked softly.

She nodded. Braced herself for it.

'Why did you hire her?'

It was so completely unexpected that she actually answered him. 'She needed a stable job with someone who wasn't going to punish her for trying to be a good mother. Someone who could give her the support she needs financially. Someone other than you, I mean.'

Little lines wove themselves into the skin between his eyebrows. 'You... You did this for her stability? For my nephew's?'

And maybe because she reminds me of you.

But she only shrugged. 'I did it because we can all use flexible employers. Employers who are understanding of family responsibility. I didn't have that when Kian died, so I thought I'd pay it forward.'

'You didn't have to,' he said slowly.

'I know.'

There was a pause. 'I think you did it for me.'

'I...did...*not.*' It was half-scoff, half-splutter. 'I *did* it,' she emphasised, 'because I knew she could use the help and she wouldn't accept it from you.'

'Yeah, but there are plenty of people out there who could use that kind of help.' He stuffed his hands into his pockets, his eyes intent on hers. 'And there are plenty of people out there who could help her. She *had* a job.'

'Not a very good one.'

'You wanted me to have peace of mind while I was gone,' he continued, ignoring her.

'You're giving yourself too much credit.'

'She didn't tell me until I saw her this past week, you know.'

'What?' she asked. 'Why? I thought she would—' She broke off when she saw his smirk. 'No!' she said again, even though it was kind of pointless.

'I can't tell you how much it means to me,' he said, serious now.

She shook her head. 'Not everything I do is because of you, Tyler.'

'No,' he agreed. 'But some of what you do is

because of me. I know that because some of what I do is because of you.' He paused. 'Like taking leave less than a month into my new job so I can tell you in person that I'm sorry.'

She didn't want to hope. Refused to on principle. He had hurt her.

But she had hurt him, too. She could see it in his eyes, in the way he carried himself.

So she stayed where she was, rooted to the spot by a responsibility she didn't feel to anyone but her family.

'I'm sorry, Brooke.' He took a step forward. 'That night… I asked for something I had no right to ask for. I panicked. I thought that if I asked you to go with me, I wouldn't be leaving you behind. Like my dad.' He shifted. 'It wasn't until you told me to listen to you that I realised… Well, I saw I was being like my dad anyway. Forcing you to acccpt a decision I'd made without considering your perspective.'

She hadn't even thought about why he'd asked her to go with him. She'd been so fixated on the fact that he had. Now, she felt guilty. Because it was so obvious that his reaction had come from fear, too. He loved her, and he didn't want to treat her the way his father had treated the family he'd claimed to love, too.

'Seems I didn't consider your perspective either,' she said softly.

'Because I was pushing you. You barely had your feet steady beneath you after everything I told you about our past. With our feelings for one another.'

'So you *have* thought about my perspective. And I... I've only realised yours now.'

'I might have thought about it, but I almost let my fears ruin...' He trailed off and took a deep breath. 'When I spoke with you that night, I was scared of being like my father. When I realised that, I was scared that I'd already ruined us. That's why I didn't contact you after that night. I thought... I thought you'd hate me.'

'I don't hate you,' she said quickly. 'I could never hate you.'

'But I shouldn't have let my fears keep me from telling you that I was an idiot.'

'No,' she agreed. 'But it gave me time to... I've figured some things out while you've been gone. I clearly still am figuring things out if what you're telling me is still able to surprise me.' She paused. 'I was scared, too. It felt like too much in such a short time because of...because of all the things you've already said.'

'I'll wait,' he said quietly. 'That's what I should have said before. My being in London doesn't have to mean the end of us. It will give me an opportunity to figure out what I want to do. It will give you the space you need to come to terms with us.'

He was desperate. She could see it in his eyes. Hear it in his tone. And she thought it was cute.

'I'll wait until you're ready,' he went on. 'Even if that means waiting after I get back from London, too.'

She pursed her lips. 'I wasn't done. How do you know I want you to wait if you don't know what I was going to say?'

He glanced down at Mochi, as if the dog had the answer. 'Please,' he said, clearing his throat. 'Continue.'

Her lips twitched. 'I was going to say that I might have made *you* feel like there was no waiting time, too. There was only then, in that exact moment. I wasn't ready to accept what was happening then, so what choice did you have?'

'You're giving me an out.'

'No,' she said honestly. 'I'm claiming my responsibility in this. I was panicking. I thought about moving away from everything I've built here and I panicked.'

'I shouldn't have—'

'Tyler,' she said sharply. 'Let me tell you that I'm sorry, too. And don't you dare tell me I have nothing to be sorry for,' she added, when he opened his mouth. 'If I'd told you that I love you, but I needed time to figure out how I could love you in light of…of everything, you would have given me that time, I'm sure.'

'I walked away.'

'And I let you.'

He frowned. 'You're making it very hard for me to grovel.'

'I don't want you to grovel. I want you to tell me that you understand. That you know if we move forward things won't always go smoothly. I want you to promise that when we make mistakes you won't punish yourself so much that you don't talk to me. And that you won't let your fears get in the way of whatever this can be.'

She paused to catch her breath, then went on because she was afraid she wouldn't be able to continue if she stopped.

'Tell me all that, promise me all that, so I can promise you I won't do any of that either. I won't use our mistakes to push you away, nor will I do it because of the intensity of what we feel for one another. I'll keep going to therapy so I can be as mentally healthy as I can be. And if you'd like to do that, too, we can even go together.'

His mouth split into a grin, but he stayed where he was. 'You go to therapy?'

She gave him a look. 'I'm a widow, Tyler. For me, going to therapy is basically like going to the spa.'

'Your sense of humour can be really morbid at times, you know that?'

She laughed. 'I'm a widow. What do you expect?'

'I promise,' he said, the soft smile on his face not dampening his sincerity at all. 'I promise every single thing you said, plus some promises of my own. I won't rush you. And we'll talk— really talk—about what we both need, even if it's hard.'

She stepped closer, clutching at his shirt with her fingers. Oh, he smelled good. And being in his space felt good. Like his proximity, his promises filled the emptiness that had been inside her since he had left that night three months ago.

'I'd like that,' she said.

His arms circled her waist. 'We can go slow.'

'We'll have to,' she said, abandoning his shirt to put her arms around his neck. 'You still have an opportunity to take advantage of in London.'

Concern flickered in his eyes. 'Are you okay with that?'

'I was the one who urged you to pursue it, wasn't I?'

'That was before.'

'Before what?'

He narrowed his eyes. Sank his fingers into her flesh. 'Before this.'

'Yeah, well, I'm coming up on some well-deserved leave, so I could probably join you in London for a while. And after that… We'll figure it out.' She rose onto her toes, bringing their lips to the same level. 'We don't have to have all the answers right now.'

His eyes softened, one of his hands leaving her waist to cup her face. 'No, we don't. Because we love one another and we'll figure it out.'

'We will,' she affirmed softly. 'Although I do have one thing we need to figure out *right now*. Do you know what it is?'

'A kiss. You want me to kiss you.'

'So stop talking and do it already.'

And he did.

* * * * *

If you enjoyed this story,
check out these other great reads from
Therese Beharrie

His Princess by Christmas
Marrying His Runaway Heiress
Her Twin Baby Secret
Island Fling with the Tycoon

All available now!